# PRAISE FOR THE NOVEL

*"I love Tiffany and her passionate heart! She had a God-inspired dream and didn't rest until it was on paper, working tirelessly to steward what God had revealed to her. Within these pages you will see the fruit of her labor and obedience. Children of the City is a novel, but the stories within it are reality for so many around the world. Be gripped and moved as you read this book, and then find what part you have to play in the fight against human trafficking."*

**-LISA BEVERE**
Messenger International
Best-Selling Author / Minister
*Kissed the Girls and Made Them Cry, Fight Like a Girl, Lioness Arising*


*"This book will stir your soul to get involved in one of our generation's greatest injustices. I love Tiffany's passion to tell this story."*

**-BRADY BOYD**
Senior Pastor, New Life Church / Author
*Addicted to Busy, Let Her Lead, Fear No Evil*


*"With compelling style and urgent pace, Tiffany pulls the curtain back on a dark world, hidden from our eyes. In this powerful work of fiction, we find disturbing realities that are truer than we want to admit. Yet, there is Hope: God is working within His world to redeem it. And we have a chance to participate in His work. So, in the end, this is not a story of Darkness but of Light. May the Light wake each of us up."*

**-GLENN PACKIAM**
Pastor, New Life Church / Songwriter / Author
*Butterfly in Brazil, Second-Hand Jesus, Lucky*


*"This is quite possibly one of the most important works of our generation. Tiffany speaks out for those who have no voice with powerfully gripping storytelling. I could not put it down until I had read the entire story. CHILDREN of the CITY is raw, real, and riveting! The story is bigger than the book and it makes its case and bleeds its cause. Most fiction books are an escape from reality; this book is a call to action!"*

**-NATE GARRETT**
National Speaker

# PRAISE FOR THE NOVEL

*"This book ROCKED me to my core! I will never look at my city or my world the same. It will open your eyes and dare you to look at what is right in front of you."*
-**Denise Rice**
International Producer of "The THORN"


*"This book highlights a topic that most of us don't know much about, but need to as Christ followers. Tiffany Pastor has a passion to see people freed from the bondage of human slavery. The story she tells will draw you in, make you aware, and hopefully move you to action."*
-**Brad Parsley**
Worship Pastor, Christ Fellowship Church in West Palm Beach, FL


*"This book holds a heart wrenching story that will open your eyes to the dark world of human trafficking and the impact one person can make when they step out of their comfort zone and open the door to love."*
-**Michelle Korth**
Founder, Executive Director of Restore Innocence

## CHILDRENofTheCITYBOOK.COM
Visit us online, and watch the book trailer.
Keep in touch on social media!

# Youth
# CHILDREN OF THE CITY

*— A Novel*

CHILDREN OF THE CITY
PUBLISHING HOUSE

**CHILDREN of the CITY: YOUTH EDITION**
Published by Children of the City Publishing House

childrenofthecitybook.com

Copyright 2014 by Tiffany Pastor.
All rights reserved.

ISBN: 978-0-9960698-2-3

Cover Art: Thinkstockphotos.com

Printed in the United States of America
First Edition 2014

*To Luke, a true Freedom Fighter, with all my love.*

*To the next generation, who is in it to end it.*

*With gratitude to those who believed in this dream, and to the One who started it all.*

The content in this book deals with mature subject matter. This version of the story has been created for teenage readers, but still addresses tragic issues in our world today.

It is advised that a parent or guardian be engaged in what a young person reads to help utilize this book as a learning tool.

# CONTENTS

# CHAPTER □ 1

>>>>>>>>>>>>>>>>>>

SILENCE was their greatest ally. It could coast through the darkness, masking every hint of alarm to the outside world. It cloaked the inner workings of every scheme, every transaction, and every level of profit. Silence was a precious commodity purchased by any means necessary. It was their safe guard, their protection. And she knew it. Celia had to partner with the silence for as long as possible, until just the right moment. She lay still, with eyes closed. Just listening.

The old 1990's brown minivan sped down an empty highway in the night. Two middle-aged men in the front seats remained silent, but the occasional glance in the rearview mirror instilled the urgency within her.

Lying on her side in the middle seat directly behind her captors, Celia peeked at the duct tape wrapped tightly around her wrists. Pain shot down her neck as the bruise on her left temple swelled. Straining to regain her senses, she recognized the men. She remembered the deal, and how her resistance had agitated the adults at the house. The older boys threw punches at the men and growled with protective anger. Fearful cries from the other children echoed in her heart. *Who will watch over them now?* she thought. She was only nineteen years old, but she had been a mother to them.

The loud rumble of the van had awakened Celia back to consciousness, and now she lay still, discreetly squinting at her surroundings. The van was dirty with random trash on the floor. Three handguns lay piled between the front seats. Her bare toes rubbed the inner vehicle wall. The men had come without warning. They took her without shoes or a coat.

"In the air by 5:00a.m.," the passenger in the front seat whispered.

"We'll make it." The driver grumbled with his eyes forward on the road. "I never miss a drop-off."

Celia trembled. All was dark and she nearly gasped as the red glowing eyes approached. Such an ominous landmark was recognizable to anyone in the city. A blue, ferocious bucking bronco loomed with its front legs frozen in the air. His wild mane and haunting glare commanded fear into the night sky. The van curved to the left as they passed the daunting statue and the white rooftops at Denver International Airport came into view. Only a few minutes remained before her last opportunity for survival.

They drove to a smaller runway farther from the terminal. An airport staff member dressed in a reflective jump suit directed them to a small private plane. A short ladder hung by hinges at the door of the aircraft. Two suited men waited.

As the vehicle slowed to a halt, Celia saw a distant glow that spilled through a wall of windows several stories up. Travelers sipped coffee by the windows. She had been silent, but now if she could just scream loud enough, draw their attention, maybe her freedom was in reach.

The driver slammed the vehicle door behind him and quickly marched to the suited men. Still in the passenger seat, the other man lusted over Celia's seemingly unconscious body.

"Too bad we don't have more time for you tonight," he said as he stroked her upper thigh. He jerked his position forward at the sound of the driver's cursing. He stepped out into the cold, and they both counted cash in an envelope. Celia's heart raced. Her arms stretched forward as both feet nudged one of the guns closer. The men's muffled voices argued over the division of their earnings. Her sweaty hands grabbed the gun and hid it in her pants by the front zipper. She slowly planted her feet on the floor of the van, and poised her fists for leverage. *Breathe,* she thought. *Remember to breathe.*

The side door slid open. With all the passionate rage she could muster, she leapt past the thieves, smacked one of them with her taped fists, and roared with all her might. Both men fell backward to the ground. The cold pavement ripped at her bare feet, and she stumbled in her landing, but with clumsy haste she pushed forward in desperation. Celia screamed uncontrollably and sprinted across the landing strip toward the terminal building.

With her wrists still tied, she grabbed the gun and fired twice straight in the air. The clamor of the four men in pursuit behind her, added to her determination. *Who will help them? Who will help them?* She pictured the children left at the house.

"Help! Please!" She shrieked with her eyes on the windows above. How quiet that world was. It was as if she was drowning in a vast ocean, and her limbs flailed and reached for the surface. Silenced bullets whizzed past her and bounced off the ground near her feet. An exterior door was now in sight, and hope filled her heart.

Whack! A fist struck the back of her neck.

The blow hurled her across the pavement. The gun flung from her hands and landed out of reach. Celia whimpered as her cheek slid across rough gravel. Her toes and elbows were bleeding from the fall. She lay still and noticed, once again, the silence. It was back. They were back. Their footsteps drew closer, and only a cold, whistling breeze accompanied them. *Who will help them? Who?* She twisted to look over her shoulder as the menacing shadows approached.

"The gunshots! Someone heard them, so you better run," she yelled while crawling on her knees toward the gun. "You can't keep me silent anymore! Help! Someone will come! Help!"

The four men spread out around her. Their lack of response and emotion was alarming, and she screamed all the more. One of the men cocked his head to the side.

"Gunshots? Did you guys hear any gunshots?" He asked. The men shook their heads with brazen confidence. The man cracked his knuckles and stared down at her.

"That's funny, nobody heard anything," he said. "What about you?" The airport staff that had directed the traffickers' vehicle approached.

"Nope, sorry. No one on our team saw anything either. I think a large jet just got its wings up in the air, and that can be pretty noisy. I am sure someone just misheard."

Even as fear crept in, a stubborn ballad rang in her heart. *Who will help them?* The leader spoke again, this time with a venomous edge that cut through each word.

"You see, little lady, no one hears you. No one sees you. I have my boys here. We look out for each other. But you, Celia, you are invisible, and no one cares." With one last attempt, she sprang with arms outstretched across the void between her and the gun on the ground.

# ⟫⟫⟫⟫⟫⟫ CHRISTMAS 1994

"We're having a baby!" The sound of gasps rippled across the formal dining room. Kayla felt the rush of hot blood sweeping up and down her body and it took great effort not to choke on her mouthful of potatoes. Her mother, Regina, immediately jumped up with a delighted squeal, knocking the chair down behind her. Kayla's father, Rex, couldn't seem to move a muscle or even blink an eye, and her brothers, Ricky and Robby, also sat frozen with plastered smiles on their faces. Regina jumped, giggled and hugged on her oldest daughter's neck. Rachel and Ryan were newlyweds, and their big news came as joyous shock to all in the family. Joyous to all but Rachel's younger sister, Kayla, who slouched in the dining room chair.

"This is the best Christmas gift we could ever get!" Regina said. The boys gave Ryan a hug and a little jab in the shoulder. Rex, the great patriarch of the family, ran to get wine from the pantry. He came back with stemware in his hands and the teenage boys helped him open the bottle. As the cork popped, Rex distributed glasses to everyone except Rachel, the mommy-to-be. Regina filled her daughter's glass with milk.

"There is no greater gift in life than the blessing of children," Rex said with a twinkle in his eyes. Kayla peered around the room. Rachel, was the oldest and apple of her dad's eye. She beamed with her hands gently rested on her abdomen, and sat beside her husband, Ryan. Robby, the second-born, was the athletic all-star, and her little brother, Ricky, often had a joke or silly impersonation that made the family laugh. Kayla looked down in her lap as she remembered the fight that took place earlier that afternoon.

"I'm not going!" Kayla yelled at her father from the top of the stairs. Rex stood at the front door and his arms waved with each exclamation.

"Don't you talk to me like that! We always go to church on Christmas Eve. It's what we do! Now, get dressed, and don't make us late. Your sister is on the way, and you know how important this is to your mom."

"Come on, Kat-Kat, stop being such a witch! You're always upset about something," Robby said through his bedroom door down the hall.

"Shut it, Robby! You don't know anything," Kayla said as she paced the hallway. Robby popped his head out the door. He struggled with his necktie, and leaned in her direction.

"You know what? Don't even bother coming, no one wants you there anyway. You're just an embarrassment to our family."

"Cut it out, Robby!" The youngest brother, Ricky, stepped into the doorway, and shoved Robby's shoulder. "Kayla, we do want you…"

"Whatever!" Robby ignored his brother and focused on Kayla. "Kat's a screw up and everyone knows it."

"What is that supposed to mean?" she asked as she stalked toward the door.

"Stop the fighting!" Rex interrupted. He stomped halfway up the stairs. "Boys, get to your room. Kayla, I've had enough of you, now get dressed."

"I'm telling you, Dad, there's no freaking way you are going to get me to go to a church tonight. Virgin birth, or not, I don't care. It's boring, and stupid. Everyone there is totally fake, and just sits around judging people all the time. The only reason you want me there is to make it look like our family has it all together, and we don't." Kayla slammed her bedroom door shut.

"Well, you will be eating dinner with the family when

we get back, so don't think you can act like this all night! Your mom has slaved over dinner and I won't let a spoiled brat like you ruin it!"

Just hours later, the feud was ignored, and Rex boasted with pride.

"I have been so lucky to have a great family, and an especially beautiful daughter in you, my dear Rachel. Ryan, you have truly become a part of this family. We are so happy for you and for us. Now, I won't get in trouble when I call your mother 'Grandma,'" Rex said with a belly laugh. The others laughed and raised their glasses together.

"Here's to a new baby! The first grandbaby in the Barrington household! May there be many more ahead!" The glasses clinked and everyone cheered the traditional "Hear Hear!" Kayla blinked her eyes and shook her head. The rest of the evening was filled with laughter and stories. Regina rubbed Rachel's tummy, and Rex drank more alcohol. After the newlyweds left, the house was quiet. Regina had a sparkling wink in her eye while tucking each of the teenagers in bed. As Regina sat on the side of Kayla's bed, she brushed the soft brown wisps of hair away from her daughter's forehead, lightly stroking her cheeks. In that dark room, Kayla agonized over the recent months and ached over telling her mom. Instead, a few tiny tears rolled down her cheeks.

"It's a happy day, and you're upset about your own..." Regina said in a whisper, but ended in a stutter. Regina sighed aloud and slipped out of the room. Kayla reached over to a pile of stuffed animals at the bedside on the floor. She grabbed a ragged old teddy bear that had come home from the hospital where she was born. She clutched the soft bear and used his ears to dry her cheeks. Just before drifting to sleep, Kayla slid her fingers underneath the pillow and pulled out her journal.

By the light of the moon, she scribbled on the paper.

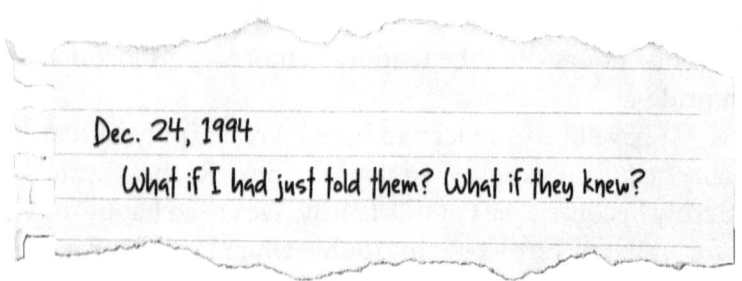

Dec. 24, 1994

What if I had just told them? What if they knew?

The pen fell out of her hand and she was already dreaming as she finished.

*A bright light shone over her and the sounds of voices echoed eerily. Her body felt heavy and lay flat in the bed as though she had been paralyzed. People were working busily around her, but she couldn't quite see what was going on.*

*"Here we go. Almost there, everyone work with me," a familiar voice said. Then, soon after, the cry of a newborn baby soared through the room. "Here he is! He's arrived!" Kayla's vision was fuzzy but a warm light glowed as the man lifted a tiny naked baby in the air. The newborn's persistent cry was like a delicate baa of a sheep. All Kayla could do was smile at him. Nurses looked over at Kayla and rushed to her side. Darkness grew again, like a fading flame that had lost oxygen to feed it. The cry of the little lamb echoed in the black.*

Thirteen years later, Kayla jerked awake, gasping for breath. The room was dark, and she felt the bed stir next to her. The neon numbers on the clock lit her room. 5:00am. *Still time to sleep*, she thought, *as long as I don't pick up where I left off.* Since the Christmas Eve of 1994 when Rachel announced the pregnancy, this mysterious dream had awakened her in the night hundreds of times. Kayla patted the lump next to her.

"Sorry, Jack, just the same old dream," Kayla said. She rolled over and hugged the neck of her black Labrador nestled in the sheets alongside her teddy bear.

Initially, Kayla thought the recurring dream was a sign that Rachel would have a boy, so she shared the dream with the family. A few months later when Rachel had a baby girl, her older brother, Robby, chastised her.

Rachel and Ryan named their daughter Rudy. In a family where everyone's name started with an "R," it seemed that even Baby Rudy was calling Kayla the outcast. Kayla's name was given simply to receive a hefty inheritance from their cantankerous Great Aunt Mildred. Kayla was the name of the great aunt's cat, and the old woman wanted the name to live on, even at the cost of her life's fortune. When Kayla's brother, Robby, heard the story behind Kayla's name, he pranced around the house purring at her. The nickname "Kat" became the siblings' way of condescending over her.

This new baby was perfectly adorable, except that when Kayla held her for the first time Rudy screamed at a deafening decibel and could only be consoled by her mother. Anyone else would not have taken it personally. Babies cry, that's what they do. But every time Kayla tried to hold little Rudy and the infant wretched out a murderous sound, it stripped away another bit of her heart.

Kayla's hidden past had left her estranged from every little girl she met, and when Rudy was born, it intensified the pain and insecurity. A little girl's fairy-like laughter sent chills up Kayla's spine. Currently, though, the inner war was at rest and ignored.

It was 5:30a.m. Kayla sat up and rubbed her eyes with a sigh. She tickled Jack's belly and whispered in his ear.

"Hey, boy, wanna go for a run?" Jack's ears perked up, and the four-year-old pup jumped straight to his feet on the mattress.

Kayla stretched her arms and legs as she stepped onto the sidewalk and breathed in the crisp air. The sun rose, and on this early morning in May, nature burst with new life. With a leash in hand and iPod in tote, Kayla took a route downtown. The high-class business world refocused her determination. The expensive cars and lofty job titles were an inspiration. She loved the smell of coffee shops and the blooming flower arrangements that hung from the lampposts.

After graduation for her Masters, Kayla worked in an office that published a local community newsletter. It wasn't glamorous, but it sufficed for a paycheck. Kayla worked two years of odd jobs and selling advertisement space before she was hired at The Denver Post. This was a fast-paced newsroom. Phones were constantly ringing. Photographers came in with the next best submissions for the front page. Her perfectionism thrived in the high-strung environment. After three years at The Denver Post, Kayla was still stuck picking up Starbucks for the rest of the team before the staff meeting each week. If there was a menial task to be done, she had mastered it. Whether writing obituaries, classified ads, or tending to the corrections page buried in the back of the paper, Kayla just hoped that someday her work would pay off.

When Kayla returned from her jog, a missed call and voicemail waited on her cell phone. Her supervisor, Mr. Stawlings, needed her to fill in some holes on a co-worker's research for a story on government involvement in the inner city. It was mostly just resolving a few questions and getting photo releases signed for an upcoming article.

When she arrived at work, Kayla hurried through her morning email so she could tackle the morning assignment. Her supervisor tapped his fingers on the desk and sighed at the clock in her direction. Every minute she thought she might be able to leave, someone with more clout would throw a new job on her desk. Soon her stomach growled.

This day had begun with a dream so familiar and yet so mysterious. Though the vision should have warned her, the hustle of the newsroom had diverted her heart. Rarely do people wake up and say, "This is the day that will change my life." Just as with many monumental moments, she did not expect it coming. She did not expect him.

# CHAPTER □ 2
>>>>>>>>>>>>>>>>>>

KAYLA smiled and tapped her hands on the steering wheel to the beat of the radio music in her car. She couldn't shake the dream from the night before. She remembered the sound of the crying baby, and the man's voice stating, "He's arrived." *Who is this mystery kid? That baby?* After a few minutes, she looked at the street signs and realized she was lost. A pile of blank photo releases lay beside her. Kayla picked up her Mapquest directions in the passenger seat, and locked the car doors. The music on the radio faded out of range into static noise. As she looked at the dashboard, her vision realigned with a different dream altogether; a deja vu moment. She had never been in this part of town before, and yet, she knew exactly where she was. She looked down at the steering wheel and speedometer. The way the sunlight hit the car suspended her connection between reality and a recurring dream she had experienced probably a hundred times. She gasped as she looked up and hit the brakes. There was a short squeal of rubber, and the car stopped. And there he was, the boy, standing in the street. In defense, he hit the palm of his hands down on the hood of her car and yelled, "Hey!"

*It's him,* she thought. His was the face she had grown to fear in her dreams. This identity she had wondered about for years. The dream of this boy had been the first thing ever jotted down in a journal. He wore an undershirt with gym shorts and sneakers. For a brief moment, their lives intersected. He stood in front of her, staring at her through the glass. She wanted to jump out of the car and shake this boy. She wanted to beg him to leave her alone. She wanted to yell at him, and yet she wanted to hug him. Something in her felt reunited with a lost friend even though she didn't know his name. But almost immediately, the mysterious boy darted across the street into the alleyway.

Kayla pulled off the road and parked crookedly on the curb. The photo releases could wait. She ran and chased after him.

"Hey! You! Kid!" The alleys were like a maze within the inner city. The cheers of men began to echo around her. As she jogged down the dirty streets, the brick walls and graffiti hid the crowd like a dense forest. Finally, she turned the corner to an alley that was packed tightly with men of all ages huddled around some sort of featured entertainment.

She couldn't see over the shoulders of the crowd in front of her, so she squeezed past one person at a time. She received a few awkward pinches, but still pushed forward. Her eyes burned with determination. The closer she got to the action, the louder the men's enthusiasm became. Just as she was about to give up, a man standing by her side put his hand on her shoulder and yelled in her ear.

"Are you lost?"

"What's going on?" she asked.

"Will's favored to win." The man pointed at the boy from her dreams. "This is the best fight we've seen all month!"

"Will?"

"The white kid!"

Will took a hit in the jaw from an African American boy nearly three inches taller than him.

"No!" she yelled as Will fell to the ground. The front row of men served as an impenetrable boxing ring leaving the two boys alone in their duel. Both fighters were skinny teenagers wearing ragged gym shorts and sneakers. Their bare backs glistened with a mixture of sweat and alley dirt. For a moment the scene reminded her of an old school fight on the playground at recess, but there seemed to be more at stake in this battle than just childish pride.

A middle-aged man stood out from the crowd. All the others cheered for one of the boys. This particular man wore a dirty collared shirt with the sleeves rolled up; his hands were stuffed in his pockets. His eyes were locked on the fighters.

The smell of body odor filled the air. The crowd pushed in tighter as the fight continued. Will's nose bled, and when he wiped his face it smeared across his cheek. The other boy hobbled with a limp on his right foot and guarded his left ribs. He grabbed Will by the back of the neck and whispered something in his ear. Will violently pushed his opponent back and threw punches in a sloppy fury. With each strike, his intensity grew more powerful. The boy slipped backward and Will pounded his face until the boy didn't respond anymore. Finally Will's fists dropped to the floor. He looked straight up in the sky and slowly rose to his feet. He nodded at the silent man. Stepping into the boxing ring, the man grabbed Will's hand and raised it in the air.

"Will wins it all!" The man yelled with a raspy booming voice. Men rushed forward to collect their winnings. Will pulled his opponent out of the way and placed their tee shirts underneath his head. Will sat with his knees propped up by his face and the back of his head rested on the brick wall.

Kayla stared at Will for a few minutes while the crowd started to thin out. She had come this far but was gripped with anxiety. *What if he thinks I am crazy?* As the men passed the boys, a few bucks landed in Will's lap.

"Nice fight, kid."

"Keep it up, Will."

"All bets on you, kid."

She stepped backward and then her eyes locked on Will. The ringleader grabbed Will's tips adding them to his fist-ful of cash. He threw down three one-dollar bills and grumbled as he walked away.

"Get some lunch, boys. And don't be late tonight. You know Mother hates getting a late start for bed time." Kayla leaned against the brick wall hiding her from the two boys. She felt paralyzed. Before turning the corner, she heard Will coaxing the boy lying next to him. She peeked around to see a brotherly affection between them.

"Hey, man. I'm hungry. Let's go." Will patted the boy's cheek until his eyes opened slowly. The boy sat up and rubbed his head. They stumbled toward the main road. Will held the three bucks tightly wadded in his hand. Their tee shirts hung wrapped around their necks and over their shoulders.

Kayla darted down a parallel alley and ran as fast as she could to cut them off before they reached the main street ahead of them. Her high heels wobbled in the cracks of the street. As she hastily turned the corner, she gasped and halted; she was nose to nose with this sweaty boy from her dreams. He didn't react quickly or dodge her.

"Woah," he said. She leapt back and lost her footing. She hopped to catch her balance, but landed hard on the pavement. Kayla looked up at the two boys before her.

"I, uh, I am sorry. I just..." She fumbled up to her feet and straightened her shirt. Will stepped forward cautiously.

"You almost hit me with your car today," he said.

"Yeah, I'm... I'm sorry about that. Well, what were you doing in the street?" Will and the other boy glanced at one another, shook their heads, and walked past her.

"Hey! Don't walk away when I'm talking to you." Kayla quickly grabbed Will's arm and he forcefully shook her off.

"Back off! You're not my mom!" The boys walked faster. Kayla watched them from behind and took one last chance.

"Are you hungry? Three bucks won't get you very far. How 'bout I buy you lunch?" The boys stopped and looked at one another. "I'm starving. Do you like subs?" Will turned, walking briskly toward her.

"What's your problem?"

"No problem. I just... it's my lunch break, and I'm hungry, and I hate eating alone, maybe you want lunch, too. No biggie," she said.

"Are you a cop?" His eyes narrowed.

"No."

"Who are you?" he asked. She extended her hand to shake his.

"I'm Kayla." He looked at her hand and spit on the ground next to her.

"Will," he said. He looked at her silently. "What are you doing here?"

"I was just in the neighborhood," she said with a casual wave of her hand.

"No, no, no." He shook his head and rolled his eyes. "It's

not your neighborhood."

"Well, I made a wrong turn, and now I'm here. So, do you want lunch, or not?"

"Can he come, too?" Will nodded toward his oppponent. Kayla glanced over Will's shoulder to see the other boy. He slouched with his eyes to the ground. Just minutes ago, these boys battled in the alley, and now they seemed to depend on one another.

"If he comes, then I fill up my Subway frequent shopper card and get a free sub!" She clasped her hands together and held her breath. Will called to the friend behind him.

"Hey, Catch. Lunch!"

Kayla invited the boys into her car. Will sat in the front and gave directions for Kayla to the closest Subway. This franchise was not as well kept as other sub shops in a nicer part of the city. Despite the well-worn appearance, the parking lot was packed for the mid-day rush hour. The boys got out of the car and started to walk in, but Kayla stopped them before they reached the door.

"Shirts," she said. Without any argument, they dressed in their sweaty shirts. She gave a genuine "Thank you" and they headed in for lunch.

"Get whatever you want," she said with a smile. The boys salivated over every item on the menu. Both chose toasted foot-long sandwiches packed with meats and veggies. Chips and a large soda made the boys even more excited and Kayla threw in some cookies, too. Will and Catch grabbed their food and headed to a booth while Kayla paid the bill. She noticed Catch bump his elbow in Will's ribs.

"You give her whatever she wants," Catch said with a wink in his eye. "This girl's got the goods."

"Shut up." Will ripped into his bag of chips. Kayla

signed the receipt and cringed at the boys' humor. *What am I doing here?* It wasn't too late to discreetly slip out the door. *No harm. They got their lunch, and I have work to go anyway.* But when she looked at Will, and remembered the haunting dream, she knew she had to stay.

# CHAPTER □ 3

>>>>>>>>>>>>>>>>>>

CATCH and Will eagerly devoured their lunch. Kayla noticed the dirt under their fingernails, and the dark circles under their eyes. They had wiped their face with some tissues from the glove box in the car. Catch's eye was slightly swollen, and Will's left hand looked a little red.

"Shouldn't you guys be in school, or something?" The boys didn't flinch, but both answered in unison.

"Home school."

"Oh." She looked at Catch who dumped crumbs from the chips in his mouth. "So, I don't think I really met you. What's your name?"

"They call me Catch-All," he said as he slurped his soda.

"Why do they call you that?" she asked. Will leaned over with an arm around his friend's neck.

"He's Catch-All, because he's the one who can catch all..."

"...the ladies!" Catch-All flashed a wide grin and raised his eyebrows.

"Aren't you a little young for 'the ladies'?" She folded her arms across her chest. The boys sat tall, and looked down at her.

"I'm sixteen. What were you doing when you were sixteen?" Catch-All said. Kayla recoiled a bit from the boy's unknowing personal jab and pried in Will's direction.

"What about you? How old are you?"

"Fifteen," he said. He wrapped part of his sandwich in the paper lining. Catch-All slurped his drink again and got up for a refill. She looked at the sandwich that was now tucked under Will's arm.

"Don't you like the sandwich? I thought you were hungry."

"Oh, I'm full." Will shrugged his shoulders.

"Not buying it."

"Who cares anyway?" Will shoved the sandwich to the middle of the table. "Who cares if I'm going to save it for later or feed it to my dog?"

"Well, are you?" Kayla leaned in. "Your dog likes red onions and cucumbers on his sub?" Kayla and Will stared silently at one another. Catch-All slid back down in the seat.

"No, but Celia does." The corner of Will's eyes tightened at Catch's interjection.

"Oh, so who's Miss Celia?" Kayla leaned back and smiled with a twinkle in her eye. Will looked down at the table, so Kayla quickly baited him. "Ya know, I have a free sub on my card to use up. Who is she? Maybe she'd like one, too?" Will's eyes lit up.

"Really?" This was the first time that Kayla's heart had really dropped for a boy in years, but not like the youthful romantic whims she had experienced before. After knowing Will for less than an hour, Kayla cared for him. She looked at this skinny kid and wanted to give him a lifetime supply of sub sandwiches. She tossed the frequent customer card across the table. It slid right in front of Will's folded arms.

"Score!" Catch-All said. "Celia's his girl."

"She's not my girl. She's my sister," Will said. Kayla looked into the hidden tenderness of this rough boy. For a moment, she saw a younger version of her little brother, Ricky.

"Your sister?" Kayla looked to Catch-All, who tapped his fingers on the soda cup.

"Well, sort of his sister. She's really his…"

"Sister!" Will said. "She's not feeling good. I just thought I'd bring it home for her."

"Home? Where's home?" she asked. Catch-All slouched in his seat, looking down in his lap. She couldn't figure out if he was embarrassed or scared. Will stood up and pushed Catch off the bench of the booth.

"Thanks for lunch. Gotta go," Will said. Kayla wasn't going to let them leave without more answers. She grabbed the Subway card and jumped in front of him.

"Don't forget Celia's lunch." She waved the reward card in the air. Will gently took the free lunch card in his hand. "Why don't you let me bring it to her? Show me where you live."

"Yeah, Will, that's a great idea! Bring the Mrs. home to Mommy!" Catch laughed and slapped Will on the back.

"Shut up, man! Sorry, K, maybe next time." The boys walked out the door, and Will slugged Catch-All's shoulder.

"Hey, man, what's that for?"

"I think you know!" Will said with a grin.

Kayla watched through the glass windows as the boys walked across the parking lot and disappeared down an alley. She returned to their table to collect the trash from lunch. She jumped as her cell phone rang in her pocket.

"Kayla, what are you doing? We are waiting to print over here!"

"So sorry, Mr. Stawlings. I'm on it. I'll be back soon, sir." As Kayla flipped her phone shut, she sighed loudly and hurried to the car. She sat in the driver's seat and looked to the empty space beside her. There was not one trace of evidence that Will had ever been there. He had vanished just as quickly as the abrupt ending in her dream.

After meeting Will, Kayla was subject to a dreamless sleep. From as far back as she could remember, Kayla dreamed. Most of the time, they were a trail of illogical images. As a child, she was met with laughter at the breakfast table when she shared the stories with her family. A handful of times she envisioned of a scenario she had never experienced, and weeks later, the dream would come to life. She was a dreamer. Kayla noticed the cessation of her dreams after the second night. Her concern grew on the fourth night. She didn't feel rested, and she likened it to a dark gray abyss, like floating in outer space but without the planets, stars, and awe.

On Sunday evening she plopped down on the floor in her apartment with a large bowl of ice cream. She felt out of control and it bothered her. She liked having order in her life. She liked the predictability of her story. Will had ruined it all, and she could not stop thinking about him .

"This is dumb." She shoveled ice cream into her mouth. Across the room Jack was lying on his belly with his chin resting on his front paws. "Dumb, dumb, dumb." She said shaking her spoon at the dog. "My life was fine before this. This kid… maybe I feel bad for almost hitting him with the car. Well, it wasn't really my fault! He wasn't looking either." She sat and ate her ice cream. "I was fine before. What's the big deal? Now I have an answer to that weird dream. It was probably just a random déjà vu moment so that I wouldn't have actually run the kid over. That's all, right?" She looked over and saw her dog asleep on the couch.

"I'm talking to my sleeping dog." She scraped the last spoonful before rinsing the bowl in the sink. Emptiness struck her heart, and she ached for a friend.

She sat down at her desk. With her hands pulled back behind her head, she spun around on her office chair, her feet in the air. She stopped and gazed at her bookshelf; a tattered paperback caught her eye. She tipped the book out of its hold on the shelf and flipped the pages. A faded ultrasound photo served as a bookmark and brought back memories of a dimly lit waiting room.

## ⟫⟫⟫ SEPTEMBER 1994

Sixteen-year-old Kayla held the ultrasound picture in her hands. Perfection and innocence filled the little profile. Pulling out her copy of *A Streetcar Named Desire*, she stuck the picture in the book, and placed her hand on the slow movement in her belly.

"Are you scared?" Carrie whispered with her head leaned toward Kayla. Though they had met only that morning at the clinic, the newfound camaraderie, as patients, was priceless. They sat beside one another in the waiting room chairs. Carrie, just one year older than Kayla, had a bubbly personality full of energy that sang through her voice and her graceful poise. Blonde curls fell over her shoulders, and she glowed with striking beauty. Her gentle spirit disarmed and drew in every woman around her. Kayla felt grateful they were walking through this day together.

"Terrified." Kayla leaned forward with an elbow on her knee and her forehead propped in her fist. "But what other choice do I have? It's such a mess." Carrie's shoulders hunched and her chin cast a shadow on her belly. "What about you? Are you scared?" Kayla asked.

"Sometimes." Carrie placed her hand on Kayla's back. "But I think I am just ready to get my life back. Ya' know? Isn't that fair? I just want my life back." Kayla looked up; tears formed in Carrie's big blue eyes.

"You're right. You don't want to lose everything ahead of you just because of... because of this," Kayla said. Carrie's brow relaxed.

"Yeah." Carrie nodded. "You're right. It's OK."

Shaking her head, Kayla slammed the book on her desk. A journal leaned over in the empty space from the play she had just removed. Kayla nonchalantly opened the journal. Her eyes fell to a page with scribbles and doodles. A lump lodged in her throat as her jaw locked. She propped her elbows on the desk and held her forehead up with her palms.

Nov. 9, 1994

For two nights I had a dream. I was moving. Sort of gliding, I guess. Dashboard.

I think I was driving somewhere, but it wasnt my car, it was totally different from mine. The sun was bright and I was distracted by a static noise on the radio. The noise was piercing and I just wanted it to stop. When I looked up, I saw this guy. A boy. He was probably around Rickys age... was it Ricky? No, but sort of like him. But not. The boy was right there. I slammed on my brakes. His hands hit the hood of the car. And he looked me in the eyes like I had killed him. So weird.

# CHAPTER □ 4

DAYS later, Kayla found that navigating through the rough streets on the lower side of Denver was no easier the second time. Kayla tapped her fingers on the steering wheel and peered at the neglected area. Faded billboards had become a canvas for graffiti artwork, and homeless people warmed the benches at each stoplight. After about fifteen minutes of circling around the same streets, she saw something that looked out of place. Two men dressed in business attire walked across the street and headed down an alley. Kayla parked, grabbed a messenger bag purse and dashed to follow the men. She trailed the men for two streets before the sounds of the crowd emerged.

Kayla was determined to reach Will; she squeezed through the sea of men and held tightly to the messenger bag over her shoulder. Instead of pushing up to the front lines, she stayed back, hidden in the crowd. She peeked over shoulders and recognized the sleek brown hair from her first encounter in this outdoor arena. Opposing Will, was a new fighter. This boy was a much taller, Hispanic boy whose limbs appeared to be twice as long as Will's. The fighter's physique was more tone than that of the skinny white boy in the other corner. Will's movements were quick, but he was blocking more than throwing his own punches. Sweat dripped in beads. Kayla grabbed the shoulder of the man next to her.

"Who's favored?" she asked. He looked at her as if she was completely blind.

"Isn't it obvious? Hugo's gonna kill this kid! I got two hundred bucks on him!"

Kayla clenched her jaw, and gripped her fists while nervously cracking her knuckles. Hugo was faster, and his punches forceful. At one point Will ducked underneath Hugo's punch and rushed a tackle into Hugo's ribs driving him up against the brick wall. Hugo regained composure and flung Will back to the middle of the ring.

"Hugo! Hugo! Hugo!" The crowd chanted as Will lost steam. "Here comes the Hurricane now!" "Kill 'em, Hugo!" "Don't let me down now!" "Bring on the blood, Hugo!" Hugo ran toward Will, and just as his punch was about to make contact, Will's last swing nailed Hugo in the throat. Everyone groaned as they watched Hugo fall through the air. Kayla covered her mouth so as not to laugh. She looked at the ringleader who had previously been pacing in the corner. A toothy grin stretched across his face, and he slowly clapped his hands. Will panted with his face contorted. The man slapped Will's back before grabbing his hand and raising it in the air.

"And Will takes it all!" His raspy laughter was heard over the grumbling crowd. The man strutted back to his post and counted his winnings in front of everyone.

"Great fight, 'eh boys? That's worth the trip out here... You'll have to win your money back next week." With a wave of his cash, he enticed the disgruntled men. Kayla slipped behind a corner and listened for the man to leave. Once again, Will sat slouched in the dirty corner. He didn't receive any tips this week. The ringleader tossed two dollars in Will's lap.

"You're short!" The boy raised his hands at the man. With a sharp turn toward Will, the leader smacked the boy on the head. In a hunched squat down to Will's level, the man grabbed his head and yelled in his ear.

"You were late! You were one shot from losing, and I don't like that kind of pressure."

"But I made you a lot of money today. How am I supposed to eat off of two bucks?" Will crouched with his head close to the ground.

"Correction: I made the money today. You just barely survived." The man walked away and stuffed his money back in his pockets. "Check out the dollar menu at BK."

Kayla waited until the man was gone. Will had not moved, still curled up against the brick wall. His shoulders flinched as she turned the corner.

"Some fight," she said. His eyes dropped and he pulled his legs closer.

"What do you want?" He wiped his face with the palm of his hand. She kneeled beside him and looked at the two dollars between them.

"I thought you might be hungry." She pulled two sub sandwiches from the messenger bag. "Let's get outta' here." She braced his arm and pulled him to his feet. Will looked around each direction in the alley.

"Where are we going?" He asked with a tremble in his voice. Will shrugged her arm off of him and walked independently.

"There's a park a few blocks down. We can eat there. I only have thirty minutes left before I have to be back to work."

The park was built in the mid 1980's and a few of the rusted metal swings were broken and hanging from one chain. Patches of green grass were mixed among the age-worn playground equipment and hard, packed dirt. Kayla found a spot of grass large enough to fit their picnic. She sat down with her legs crossed and unloaded their feast. Her messenger bag was full of water bottles, a large bag of chips, apples, cookies and sub sandwiches. Will pulled off his dirty shoes and wiggled his toes in the soft blades of Kentucky blue grass.

The sun was warm with the backdrop of a blue Colorado sky and a gentle breeze. Kayla had waited a whole week to see this boy again, yet found herself speechless as they ate. Will guzzled the water and food. Kayla marveled at his resilience. She grimaced at the thought that maybe he had not eaten this much since she last bought his meal.

What began as a charitable donation for a needy kid became a regular date to which both parties eventually looked forward. The boy intrigued Kayla, and it felt good to get outside of her normal funnel of self-concern. On Wednesdays, Kayla treated Will to lunch at Subway. For a few bucks she bought him a twelve-inch sub, chips, drink and cookie. She loved watching him pick out all the ingredients. He loaded the sandwich with cheese, meats, and every other addition he could get. Ranch dressing was his new favorite.

This ritual continued throughout the entire summer. Will was eager and quietly grateful, but their meeting always came with a stern stipulation. He insisted that she meet him at the corner and never come to the fights again. She couldn't take a long lunch break so each week was like a new installment of a 30-minute sitcom television show.

Little by little, Kayla learned more about Will. The first three months he refused any information regarding his home life. Finally in late July, he slowly opened up. He was an orphan since before he could remember. He never knew his parents. He lived in a house full of orphans of many ages with both boys and girls. Whenever Kayla pressed for details, Will diverted the conversation. Sometimes he was smooth and laughed it off or added a sarcastic jab. She was still winning his trust, and she depended on the fresh lunch as her bargaining chip to keep him coming back.

They enjoyed laughing together as they shared silly memories and embarrassing stories from their past. They discussed anything from favorite scenes in movies to solving the city's traffic issues in a twenty-minute conversation. Will had fewer manners and more gall. He effortlessly blurted out the most personal questions with food hanging from his mouth. Kayla felt more comfortable and more transparent with him than she had with anyone in years. When he asked her the hard questions, she never feared or worried over his response. For the first time in more than thirteen years, she felt truly connected with someone.

"If you could have one re-do in life... like, you could go back in a time machine and change your life, what would you do?"

"Well, I think I would have run you over that day I met you. It sure would have saved me a lot of lunches," Kayla said. Will mockingly threw is head back in the air and pretended to laugh obnoxiously at her sarcasm.

"Ha ha ha! You are so funny! Ha!" Will continued eating his chips. Kayla put her sub down on the table, and scratched her head.

"Well, what about you?"

"No, no. Don't be dodging me." Will folded his arms and cocked his head. Kayla exhaled and looked away from his persistent stare.

"I had an uh, a procedure done that… Well, it was a termination… sort of like a procedure that…ended, umm," Kayla fumbled and began crumpling her trash in a tight ball. Will leaned closer.

"Lay it out."

"Well, I didn't want to give it up, but I just..."

"An abortion?" Her head dropped and she stared at the table.

"Yeah." She whispered, but could not look at him. "How did you…"

"Where I come from, that junk happens all the time." They both sat quietly. She sipped her drink. "So, how old were you?" He said.

"Sixteen. Can we just talk about the Broncos or something?"

"Wow." He ignored her request. "So, why would you want to take it back? What would you do over?"

"I guess I always wondered, like, what if this baby… actually, they said it was a girl, so, what if she was destined to do something great. Ya know? Like, what if she was going to be President of the United States or an astronaut, or a Nobel Peace Prize winner? What if she was going to cure cancer? What if she was really special, and now the world is missing out on her achievements?" Will was silent, and his brow furrowed. "What's wrong? Are you mad or something?"

"Nah, it's just, well… yeah." He hesitated for a moment, but then leaned forward with angst in his eyes. "What if she wasn't gonna be nothin' special? At all. No awards, no curing cancer, nothing. What if she was just plain normal? What if she struggled in school like the other kids and was just like everyone else? You said you regret it. You would do it over if she was really special." Will leaned back in his chair and folded his arms. "What if the only thing special about her was that she was yours?" He paused and looked down at her with his eyebrows raised. His nose crinkled a bit.

"What then?" He spoke louder and his eyes got wider. "Does that change everything? What's the difference between your genius kid and the kids in this city who just gotta fight to survive?"

"Why don't you ever take me to see your place?" she asked.

"What? It's not the place where you bring a girl home to meet the folks, ya know."

"Don't flatter yourself, kid. I'm not about to be brought home by you. I just thought it would be nice to see where you live. Maybe I could meet Celia, and meet the people who own the place."

"Yeah, I'm thinking that's a 'No,'" he said flatly and crumpled his trash. "Trust me, my life is nothing like yours. You gotta be crazy tough to roll with me, and sorry, but that's not gonna fly here. If you think you got strings attached to me over a sandwich, then forget it."

"OK! OK! I'm sorry! Don't get hateful on me. I just want to know you. Here you know my deepest darkest secrets, and what do I really know about you?" His eyes narrowed. Kayla felt torn between deeper curiosity and shame for pushing him past his limit.

"Just 'cuz you tell me about some abortion doesn't mean we're tight. You got that? I've seen way worse. You don't know pain. Or life on your own. We're not the same. My life may be worth crap to you, but at least I'm livin' it." He abruptly tore away and flung the glass door open with his fists.

# CHAPTER □ 5

>>>>>>>>>>>>>>>

IN the following days, Kayla's inner battle felt ragged and raw. Her mornings were filled with stubborn and prideful defensiveness. Replaying the blowup with Will only enraged her more. Lunch breaks at work were spent hashing it out in her journal.

Sept. 9, 2008

What does he know anyway? I KNOW pain. I know rejection, and failure. He's not the only one who's ever been hurt before. He makes me crazy. Here I try to do something nice- feed this kid out of the goodness of my heart, and this is how he repays me? Whatever! Here I am paying for lunches week after week, keeping this kid alive, and he's just... UNGRATEFUL!!!

——> Well, not anymore. No more.

By evening, the gentle glow of the moon calmed her hard edge and allowed for more sober reflection. Will's harsh words left her wounded, and she didn't know how to heal.

Saturday wouldn't have been an easy day regardless of the argument with Will earlier in the week. On this day each year, secret remorse clouded Kayla's mind. As she mourned the loss of her daughter, she was reminded of how it impacted all her relationships. Following the procedure, she felt foolish being betrayed by her boyfriend at the time. Trusting men in her life became an impossible challenge. Resentment toward young girls isolated her from her own family as she struggled to remain close with her sister and niece. She felt disconnected from other women her age, especially those who were pregnant, and she feared their judgment. Though, none of these topped the betrayal at home.

Roughly eighteen months after the procedure, Kayla was approaching her high school graduation. It had been a hard junior and senior year since the abortion, but she was glad to start a new season. The hype over the new grandbaby made Kayla eager to get out of the house. Regina offered to throw a graduation party inviting friends and family for a cookout dinner. Kayla and Regina sat in the kitchen at the breakfast bar writing down a guest list.

"Who's Carrie Floto?" Regina reviewed the handwritten list that Kayla had put together. Carrie had been the only empathetic friend Kayla trusted through the recent months. They had walked into the clinic as strangers, but walked out as sisters. Carrie knew, and she listened.

"Oh, she's just a friend I met last year. We have a lot in

common." Regina didn't think twice of her daughter's noncha-
lant response and moved on through the list.

"OK, so we've got the Porters, my sister and her kids,
Johnsons, Whitmires, which means we definitely can't forget
the Murrays or Helfrich clan," she said penciling in the addi-
tions on the bottom of the list." And then Memaw and Pops, of
course your friends from school, and…" Regina's eyes fell to the
bottom of the list. "Gregg Cole? Really, honey? You don't really
want him to come, do you?"

"Mom, he was an important part of my life, and, anyway, I want him to see how good I look in my new outfit, and
how happy I am without him."

"Yes, dear, but is this really necessary? I mean he treated
you so badly when you had the abor--" Regina cut her state-
ment short, but the unintended confession grabbed Kayla's attention. Regina bit her lip and doodled on the guest list.

"What?"

"Oh nothing, Kat, if you want to invite him that's just
fine. It's your party, so you can do whatever you want."

"What did you say?" Kayla spoke in a slow monotone
voice.

"Oh, nothing, sweetie, now what sort of food do you
think we should serve?"

"You knew about this? How did you know?"

"How did I know? Kat, I'm your mother. You think I
can't tell when my girl is pregnant? I'm not that dense! You were
always out with Gregg doing God-knows-what. Baggy clothes,
swollen boobs, and your hormones were off the charts."

"They weren't that huge. Besides, why wouldn't you say
something? You knew that whole time, and you never talked to
me even once."

"I just figured you would come to me when you were

ready."

"I had an abortion, Mom! Where were you? I can't believe you knew and you wouldn't say anything. You just stood by and watched your daughter…" Kayla rubbed her eyes, then repeatedly ran her hands through her hair.

"Honey, I said I was sorry."

"I just- I can't believe this! What kind of mother sits back and lets her daughter ruin her life? Why didn't you stop me? Why didn't you tell me it would be OK?"

"Kayla, be reasonable," Regina's defensive, argumentative attitude was starting to kick in. "Having that baby would have ruined your life. Ruined! Now, don't sass me or tell me I'm in the wrong. I'm not the 16-year-old who wound up pregnant."

"Honestly, I don't know what's worse, betrayal from your boyfriend or being totally abandoned by your family. Did Dad know, too? How about the boys? Was it a big family joke?"

"That's enough, young lady. You have no idea the pressures of being a parent. Don't even talk to me like I'm the villain here." Regina had reverted to her "mom voice" which was the breaking point for Kayla's temper.

"The villain? No, that's right, villains actually do something! You are a bystander. You stood by and watched your daughter blindly walk into the darkest hour of her life all alone. What? Were you worried about what the neighbors would say? Bet you didn't want to be known as the mom of a slut. How can you call yourself a mother? How can you call me your family? You left me high and dry to wallow in my own depression. I've never felt so lonely, Mom… until now." Kayla stormed out the side door of the kitchen leaving Regina sitting silently at the bar.

When Kayla returned home she packed her bags and applied for the first summer session at Denver University. She had already been accepted for the fall, but did not want to wait any longer. She didn't speak a word to her mother or father. When her younger brother, Ricky, tried to approach her, she simply slid a note under the crack of the bedroom door.

Dear Ricky,

I know you probably don't know much of what is going on around here. I just want you to know that I love you, but I have to get out of here. There's no one left for me to trust. Please don't take this personally. I just have to do this on my own.

Love, Kayla

The family attended her High School graduation and sat in the stands watching their estranged daughter walk the stage and receive her diploma. As Kayla shook the hand of her principal she heard the family cheering for her. She did not acknowledge them. Even when she wanted to reconcile, she was too stubborn to return home. She was in too deep, and she was certain that this was the only way. The family tried making contact from time to time. Rachel emailed Kayla with quick updates, but ever since that day, Kayla had not spoken to her parents. She worked her way through college and began a career, but no matter how hard she tried, it seemed that unbridled perfectionism scathed her.

Lying on the couch in her apartment, Kayla looked out the window as she remembered the many different September anniversaries over the past decade. On this particular Saturday, fourteen years after the procedure, she thought about the recent months spent giving to this boy. She had been convinced that she was a better person for buying him lunches, but the reality of her disappointment only indicated that she was selfishly expecting something in return. On occasion Catch-All had joined them for lunch, and she always cringed at his sexual jokes whispered in Will's ear. "Shoot, man, this chick's storing up for the royal treatment." "Are you sure you aren't jumping her up on the side? You can tell me, bro." Will denied the claims with a jab in his friend's side. She wrote it off as typical teenage humor. It was now obvious to her that she had kept a tab on the boy, and he had failed to pay up.

After five months, this strange new boy had changed something inside of her. Will could challenge her, and make her laugh. He had slowly grown to trust her, but there was still a wall of separation between the two of them. She had been content not knowing the details of his life, because she didn't want to actually have to care too deeply or grieve over someone else's pain. Now, as the sun was shining on yet another secret anniversary, she decided to end it with Will. Before meeting this boy, she had grown comfortable with her pain. She had enough friends on Facebook to assure that she was not agoraphobic, and she figured her depression was normal. She thrived in the delusion that she was independent, though, nothing could have been farther from the truth. *Yes, it must end,* she thought.

With a newfound confidence, Kayla swiftly shut all the drapes in her apartment. She shut out the sun and curled up within her cave of solitude and began a marathon of her favorite TV shows. *Friends, Sex in the City,* and *Seinfeld* would console her through this day. The escapism of sitcom television would usher her into a new day. Hours passed, night fell, the dog slept. Finally around midnight, Kayla's heavy eyes fell slowly as Jerry Seinfeld, with his wit and laugh tracks, continued into the night.

The roads out of the city into the suburb of Babson were completely empty. On the outskirts of Denver, Babson was much akin to Littleton or Castle Rock. She had forgotten how long the drive out to Women First Clinic really was. She didn't know what she would see when she got there, but she knew she had to go. Maybe the place had burned down. Maybe she would key the car of the doctor on site. Maybe she would hurl rocks at the windows and scream off fourteen years of anger and pain. Or maybe she could just sit in the parking lot and do nothing. Either way, she wanted it all to end. When she had left that clinic as a scared teenager on a Saturday morning, she had left something there. She was different. Something inside of her had changed. And maybe if she went back, she would find what had been lost. She drove silently in the car, remembering the faces that greeted her in the parking lot on that day.

## ⟫⟫⟫⟫ SEPTEMBER 1994

On the morning of the procedure, the clinic had been surrounded by conservative Christians with hideous posters in their hands. Relentless cries of condemnation were heard before she had stepped out of her boyfriend's car.

"Look at them, religious freaks. It figures I have to walk right past them to get in the door." Kayla pulled her purse up into her lap, and rubbed her belly.

"You'll be fine. This will all be over soon," Gregg said. Kayla's lip quivered, and she looked out the window to hide her tears.

"Please come with me," she said in a whisper. Gregg sighed and rolled his eyes.

"Don't do this, they might not give you the scholarship if I come. Just grow up, and let's move on." Gregg leaned over to kiss Kayla, but she rushed out the car door before he could reach her. After slamming the door shut, the car pealed out of the parking lot.

On that day, it had been unusually cold for Denver in September and she shivered while gulping in deep breaths of dry air. Kayla wrapped herself in her coat and rubbed her hands together for warmth while surveying the parking lot. As she walked toward the zealous protesters, the harmony of their ballad grew in sync. Some were wearing tee shirts that said "God loves new life" and others held posters that read, "God hates Abortion." Enlarged images of dead fetuses in the shape of disfigured brown blobs with blackened heads were propped up before her.

"Abortion is murder! You should be locked up on death row! Abortion is murder!" A large balding man with a priest's collar led the rally. With each booming shout, the man's face grew redder and redder. Despite the weather, he was sweating with fiery emotion. The bellow of his voice served as a booming bass in a band. All the others drew their energy from the rhythms of his boisterous howling. *Dear God, where are you? Please help.* Before finishing her prayer, the priest hurried to her side and shouted in her face.

"Jezebel! Murderer! Have you no soul?! This is irrevocable evil!"

She had hardly been able to breathe and rushed in the door at the clinic. With each step, it was as if she felt the finger of God pointing down at her with nauseated disgust and eternal disapproval.

Her eyes now strained as she hunched over the steering wheel. She looked for the right building as each traffic light approached. In fourteen years, not much had changed in the little town. She bit her lip as she turned the corner to see the sign with a new title and logo on it.

"No way." Her stomach turned as she pulled into the packed parking lot. "This cannot be happening." She stopped in front of some empty parking spots marked "Guest Parking." The cars in the lot glimmered in the sun. Stepping into the fresh air, Kayla folded her arms and leaned back against the side of the car. Faint chords of music chimed from inside as she glared at the building labeled "Worship Center." Turning back to the entrance she read the sign by the road. In a casual font with an illustrated mountain logo image, the sign read "Church on the Rock." The building was freshly painted, but there was no question she was at the right place.

Her throat tightened. Muscles tensed, and she fumed over her spoiled plans. *Are you kidding me?* Checking the time on her watch, she realized that it was right in the middle of the church service. If she broke a window now, she would likely be arrested for a hate crime. She flung her face up to the sky. The sun sent rays peeking through the white fluffy clouds, and with every bit of irreverence and gall she screamed so that the Heavens would hear her. Then she stopped. The air was still. The muffled music continued inside. Nothing changed.

Sept. 10, 2008

I think God is laughing at me. After a wasted day of nothingness, I thought maybe I could put all this behind me... only to find that the clinic is now a church. How appropriate? Now there are hundreds of people waiting there to condemn me. What started out as a dozen hateful protesters has multiplied into hundreds. Why can't they leave? All I want is one day to drain myself of all this crap and leave it back at the place where I got it. And yet, there they are... with their God... laughing...

...waiting for me to fail again.

# CHAPTER □ 6

>>>>>>>>>>>>>>

"WRITER'S challenge." The newsroom whirred with a delicate murmur of piquing interest at Pete Rivers' announcement. A writer's challenge was a rare opportunity that surfaced only when the normally gruff old man was in a cheery mood and had white space to fill. Pete was a legend in the world of journalism, with nearly 40 years in the field, national awards for his writing, sharp journalistic instincts, and over 15 years as a managing editor. He had personally hired Kayla for her position, even at the criticism of Mr. Stawlings who oversaw the department. Every intern lived for the writer's challenge with hopes of getting published and breaking into the industry over night.

"It's Thanksgiving this week, right? Well, call me crazy, but I think that most journalists neglect the whole giving thanks scenario. Call it the pace of our business, or just the realistic view of the world we live in, so let's look at this thing a little different, 'eh folks? I have some white space, and it's up for auction to the highest bidder. But here's the catch, I want you to think of the thing you have hated the most, or maybe the thing you have never once appreciated. Get up close and personal, and try to find one thing in your arch nemesis that you are grateful for. Then give me 500 words about your experience. No, no, scratch that. 350 words. Cut out the romance, and give me your raw reaction. Get it in by 2pm on Wednesday, and you might see your byline on Thursday morning." He looked around at his audience and enjoyed the moment before yelling, "Go!"

Everyone hustled across the office. Kayla remained still as she watched her eager comrades race to fill their 350 words before anyone else. Pete slowly walked back toward his office. Standing by the door, he looked her in the eyes and leaned forward.

"Go."

Though she wanted to meet his every expectation, she hated the prompt assigned. Try as she might, she could not come up with any alternative options, and she knew a drive back to Babson was in order.

Kayla's right eye twitched while she took the first step across the threshold of the glass double doors at the Church on the Rock. She half expected to see the grumpy secretary from the clinic sitting at the front desk surrounded by the early 90s décor and a wall full of colored medical files. Despite her fears, the lobby had a warm and inviting atmosphere. Where there had once been a typical office desk, there was now a welcome center with stacks of flyers and information on upcoming events. To her relief, the lobby was empty. Doors on each side of the welcome station were labeled "Worship Center" in vinyl lettering on the wall above.

Walking through the Worship Center doors she found a large room filled with a couple hundred chairs. Before, it had been a maze of hallways and operating rooms, and it was sobering to see how big the facility actually was. Kayla walked down the center aisle while taking in the aesthetics of the room. The chairs had metal frames with green cushions. The stage was three feet high with steps leading down to the main level. A round stained glass window with the mountain logo hung at the center of the back wall. Sunlight sent soft colors onto the stage floor through the stained glass.

Kayla sat on the floor in front of the stage. With her legs crossed, she hunched over and opened a new journal in her lap. Her fingertips played an impromptu beat on the clean page. The room was so quiet that she heard an echo from the constant clicking of her retractable pen in hand.

## ❯❯❯❯❯ SEPTEMBER 1994

"I know you've been through a lot today, dear, but there's just a few must holes to fill in here to get your paper work done." A young Kayla looked up at the nurse and focused her eyes on the clicking of the pen. Sue was the receptionist at the front desk and was less than thrilled to track Kayla down in the recovery room. Kayla faced forward in the reclining chair with her hands on her flat stomach.

"Last question. You never filled out the name of the fetus. Did you have a name?" asked Sue.

"Why does it matter?"

"It's just for closure, dear. It looks like your file says the fetus was a female. A lot of times this is helpful in your response to the termination."

"Blanche. Tennessee Williams wrote about a woman who lived a very pathetic existence. I always figured this woman should have been spared from her lot in life. I guess that's what I am doing today. That's what I did today," Kayla said in a flat tone. Without any response, Sue wrote the name in the file and walked away. Kayla rolled to her side. She glanced over at Carrie who was still sleeping. From that day forward, she hated the notion of closure.

"Can I help you?"

Kayla cursed under her breath. The memories had left her in such disconnect that she didn't even hear the man walk in the sanctuary. She hoped that the voice was directed to someone else. She heard feet moving toward her, but did not respond. She kept herself hunched in a ball and her eyes remained focused on the color-speckled carpet. Moments later she saw a pair of blue Nike running shoes. She waited to hear his voice again, but was surprised when she felt his hand pat her back, and in the same movement, the man turned on his heels and started back up the aisle toward the lobby.

All was quiet again, but Kayla could not refocus on her assignment. *What an idiot. He must think I'm crazy! I might as well have been curled up like a baby sucking my thumb.* Pacing the front altar area, she pored over Pete's prompt. She retraced her steps and sat in one of the green chairs. Looking up at the ceiling tiles, her imagination swept her back to the operating room. *How can I be grateful for this place?*

With a deep sigh, Kayla stood up and walked back to the lobby. She didn't see anyone and began to move toward the glass doors. Almost free. As she stepped into the lobby a man popped up from behind the welcome station. His back was to her and he was tying up plastic bags with paper waste inside. She darted with outstretched hands for the glass doors.

"Did you find what you were looking for?" Even though she wanted to sprint to the car, some amount of pride welled up and reminded her that she was, in fact, an adult and she must act like one.

"I'm sorry?" She turned toward him. His fists were still gripping the trash bags.

"I just thought that maybe…"

"Maybe, what? You could help me? Fix me? Save me?" The man's eyes softened. He looked down at the counter and at the trash.

"No, ma'am. I just thought maybe you were looking for someone. Maybe I could point you in the right direction." His brown eyes lifted to meet hers. He was a handsome man with strong shoulders, brown hair and a clean-shaven face. He wore a sky blue polo shirt, and in any other situation, Kayla would have been attracted to this man, but standing in an abortion clinic turned church, her guard was up.

"I don't really know what I was looking for." She stuck one hand in her front pant pocket and the other tightly gripped her journal at the side of her hip. Her response invited the man to engage her all the more. He walked around the countertop and took a few steps in her direction, but stopped halfway between her and the desk.

"I'm Josh." His vulnerable spirit fascinated her.

"Kayla."

"Nice to meet you." He said with a comfortable smile.

"You, too."

She wasn't going to meet him in the middle, so he took a step forward. She noticed the same blue Nike running shoes.

His faded blue jeans had a stylish rip in the knee. She didn't think that 'church people' actually wore stuff like that. *Maybe he's here like I am. Maybe he's gonna throw a rock in the window, too.*

"If you're not sure what you came for, then what did you find?"

"Huh?" Her eyebrows raised.

"You were in there a while, I figured it was long enough that you found something, maybe not what you were looking for, but something."

"I don't really know yet."

"Oh."

"I have an assignment for work, and it's due tomorrow, so I just thought I would try to find some inspiration."

"Oh! Great! I always look to God for inspiration, too! What's your assignment? Where do you work?" Now Kayla definitely regretted the seemingly innocent discourse. *Oh great! He's not throwing a rock at the window; he'll likely just throw one at me.* This was a fork in the road that generally all people approach at some point in their lives. *Will I be who I am? Or will I be who he wants me to be?* She chose the charade.

"I work at The Denver Post. I am writing an article on people's personal faith. There are so many messages out there, just thought I would come here for a fresh revelation, ya know?" She smiled back at him.

"Wow. That's really awesome. I love that. Are you going to interview people of different faith backgrounds?"

"Oh, yeah. It's nice to hear the, uh, testimony of God's great work, ya' know. Um, so yeah, it's good to get people's perspectives in the article, too." Now she was starting to feel like a fish flailing out of water. She wasn't sure how much longer she could keep up the act. She leaned toward the exit.

"Well, if you want, I could share my story, or if you wanted any help on your article, I would totally be happy to help."

"Sure. That'd be great."

"Really?"

"Yeah, I am sure it would really add to this story." His smile widened as he returned to the welcome center desk covered in trash bags.

"Great. OK, so here's my number. Call me, and we can set up a time to talk." He grabbed a pencil and flyer, flipped it over and jotted down his contact information. She took the paper and knew her little acting debut needed to end as soon as possible.

"Look, sorry, I gotta go." She turned for the door and headed out without waiting for his response.

"Have a happy Thanksgiving."

"You, too," she said.

The quiet refuge of her little black Nissan Sentra brought a sense of safety and normalcy. Nothing had been accomplished. *How am I ever going to find 350 words? What am I gonna tell Pete?*

Her stomach growled. All she could think about was a creamy, warm pumpkin latte. It was one of the indulgences accompanying the holiday season that she could not resist. Maybe Pete would accept the hot drink as a peace offering.

# CHAPTER □ 7
>>>>>>>>>>>>>>>>>>

"BARRINGTON!"

Kayla nearly jumped out of her seat when she heard her name booming from her boss' office. She hurried over with her eyes to the floor. Pete was sitting at his desk with arms folded and staring at the Starbucks drink sitting on his desk.

"Shut the door."

Pete didn't move a muscle, and she stared at the age spots peeking through his thinning silver hair. The office was so quiet that she could hear the early morning sounds of the newsroom through the closed window and door.

"What is this crap?" Pete fixed his eyes on the seasonal drink, its sweet pumpkin smell steaming through the lid.

"Well, I know you like coffee, sir, and I just figured…"

"Where are my words?"

Kayla knew that excuses would only agitate the man. When she didn't answer, Pete began ranting all the more.

"Copy, Barrington. Copy! I've got white space to fill, not my stomach. Why do I get the feeling this pumpkin crap is all

I'm gonna see from you today?"

"Sir, uhh…"

"Don't 'Sir' me!"

"Pete, you said it wasn't due until…"

"Don't give me that! I'm not an idiot. This is an excuse. I don't like excuses, Barrington. Where's my copy?" Kayla's throat tightened and she bit her lip while holding back tears.

"I don't have it."

"Why!?"

"It's a difficult assignment."

"Excuses!"

"That's all I've got, Pete." The cushioned swivel chair squeaked as Pete turned and stood. Walking over to face Kayla, Pete sighed and leaned his weight against the edge of the desk with folded arms propped above his belly. He rubbed the whole length of his face stretching his cheeks back and forth.

"What are you scared of, Kayla?" She couldn't remember any time that he had actually called her Kayla. All was quiet.

"You're better than this. You'll never get a break in this business like this."

Still quiet.

"You're running. Stop. Just face it." Pete spoke at a normal level.

"I'm sorry, Pete, I don't know what you mean."

"Even if this road's all crap. At least I am living my life, ya' know?"

"Yes, sir."

"So, do it."

"Yes, sir."

"Look at me, Barrington." She raised her head, but could barely see through her tears. Pete didn't acknowledge her emotion. "Whatever it is, go after it. Don't miss it."

*Will!* She thought. He was it. She nodded her head, and Pete cracked the tiniest hint of a smile. He promptly turned and took a long swig of the hot drink sitting on his desk. He closed his eyes and swallowed it slowly.

"Now, that's good," he said as though stepping into a completely different scene with a facetious smile on this face.

Sitting back at her desk she tried to remember what project had been interrupted by Pete's pep talk. A calendar hung to the right side of her cubicle. She looked at it and hoped to find her way back into the grind of deadlines for the day. *Wednesday. Today is Wednesday?*

It was 11:52a.m. and Kayla was going to make a run for it. She had not seen Mr. Stawlings all morning and it was not likely that he would poke around in the next few minutes. Kayla grabbed an armful of files, papers, and purse. Though trying to act casual, she felt light and giddy. Please let him be there. I don't want to miss him. The elevator was almost in reach when her office phone rang. She heard Evan, in the cubicle next to her, answer her phone.

She dashed back to her desk, and watched across the newsroom as Evan, with his back toward her, was jotting down a message. She wanted to whack him upside the head but thought better of it since he was kind of new to the office. She arrived behind him just as he dropped the phone back in its holder.

"Evan! What are you doing?"

"Well, well, well! Miss Kayla, who is he? Don't tell me we are office neighbors and you never told me about this guy." Evan leaned against the cubicle partition. He was a gangly twenty-two year old, fresh out of college, who landed his job out of completely unmerited luck. He loved any amount of attention that Kayla would give him. She snatched the memo off her desk. The note simply had the name "Josh" at the top and a phone number underneath.

"Seriously, Evan, will you just stick to answering your own phone? This is just a lead on a story, OK?" She waved her hands sending Evan back to his desk. She checked her watch while throwing the office phone on her shoulder and dialing the number. "I don't have time for this!" She glared at Evan before turning her back toward him and sitting down in her chair. The phone rang two times and a woman answered.

"Church on the Rock, this is Dee Ann, how can I help you?"

"I'm sorry, I, uhh, I just missed a call from Josh, and he left this number."

"Oh sure thing, Pastor just stepped out for lunch, but I can forward you to his voicemail."

"Oh no, no…" The woman connected her to the office extension and she heard Josh's voice on the message.

"Hi, this is Pastor Josh…" Her jaw dropped. *He's a pastor? I lied to a pastor? I am totally gonna fry for this!* The message continued, "…and I'm sorry I missed your call. Please leave your name and number, and I will be sure to get back with you. Thanks!" She knew that Evan was eavesdropping. When the voicemail beeped in her ear it was as if she turned into a completely different person.

"Hi, Josh, this is Kayla Barrington. I am so sorry I missed your call. I had just stepped away from my desk. I would love to chat with you, so please give me a call." Kayla coolly gave her personal cell phone number and bade goodbye with a smile. When she hung up the phone, she turned toward

Evan with a vengeful look in her eye. The message made her appear confident and happy. It drove Evan to madness with curiosity. He certainly didn't have to know that she was leaving a message for a preacher.

"Gotta run," she said. Evan followed Kayla with boyish intrigue.

"Do you have lunch plans? Uhh, I mean… can I come? I mean…"

"Bye, Evan." There was no man who could get between her and Will at this moment. Not Evan, not a preacher, not her boss. Nobody.

The streets were relatively bare, but the sight of white men in business attire meandering on the sidewalks was a sure sign that the fight was on. On Wednesdays, their greed and hidden aggression lured them to the gambling fiesta. Droves of them were hidden behind the ominous brick buildings, but if they all rushed out at once it would draw attention to the underground club. The men staggered themselves and walk in small groups down the sidewalks. After a summer of lunches with Will, she recognized familiar faces making their way to the fight scene. This time, though, the men were walking away from the alley that she had been to before. She checked the clock on the dashboard of the car. She was a little later than she intended, but she was sure she couldn't have missed anything yet.

She parked the car, and more traffic in the alley was moving in the wrong direction. The working class men were now leaving. They grinned with crooked teeth and licked their lips at her as she passed them. She disregarded any worry over being noticed, and her figure-flattering business attire was not going to help her blend in anyway. The men made no effort to move aside as she walked upstream. She ignored the disgusting feel of their bodies intentionally brushing up against her.

Just as she was about to turn the corner, a man unknowingly stepped in front of her. She let out a breathy gasp and instinctively apologized. He tipped a filthy hat in her direction and took a glance at her chest before brushing past her. The dirty red suspenders were a dead giveaway, and his pockets were bulging with hidden cash. It was the leader of the pack. This was the man who had been managing Will. She didn't know anything about him, but she hated him still. She hated him on Will's behalf. Turning the last corner, she felt a new wave of heat. All the energy and sweat had culminated into a nauseating stench hovering over the makeshift boxing ring. More striking than the smell was the unconscious young man lying on the other side of the ring.

The alley was empty and he was alone. She looked around and hoped that Catch-All would arrive to help her, but there was no one.

"Will!" She fell to her knees beside him and shook his shoulders. Grabbing his cheeks between her hands she bent down in his face. "Will, it's me! Are you there? Can you hear me? Will?" She called out his name in every possible way she could think of. She tried to boss him with authoritative urgency, she tried pleading, she tried optimistically wooing him, she whispered in his ear and shouted in his face. Nothing worked. If he was breathing, she could hardly tell. She reached for the cell phone in her back pocket only to realize it was left on the driver's seat of her car. She called out his name over and over as though it were both a curse word and a cry of hope. Tightly gripping Will's shoulders, she bent over to bring her nose nearly to his chest. She broke a fourteen-year boycott and prayed.

"God, even if you hate me, I need your help. If you're out there, please help Will. Please, God. Please."

Kayla felt weary as she sat in the filth. The sun shifted and a shadow stretched a chilling blanket across them. The breeze raised goose bumps all over Will's uncovered upper body, and in a weak jolt she heard a wheezing gasp of air. She looked up to see his chest rising with air.

"Will!" She moved so he could get a look at her. His left eye was so puffy that he could barely open it.

"We have to get you to a doctor. I can take you to the ER." She helped him to his feet.

"Huh? No! No doctors! I'm fine."

"But Will, we have to get you some help."

"No! No doctors!"

"Will? Seriously, I think your nose is broken, and you need an X-Ray."

"No! You wanna help? Then leave me alone!" Will struggled to his feet and grabbed his shirt on the ground.

"What are you afraid of? Let's talk to the orphanage, I'm sure they'll want you to see a doctor."

"No! They don't know about the fights. They don't need to know. This is just extra cash. Doctors will just blow my cover."

"That shiner on your face is what's gonna blow your cover."

Will started walking down the alley.

"Where are you going?"

"I'm hungry." He spoke over his shoulder.

"Me, too." She called after him, but he kept walking. "OK, forget the doctor. Just come eat with me." His walk slowed down a bit. He looked up at the sky, sighed, and started the walk back toward her.

"What time is it?"

"Almost 1:00."

"OK. Let's eat."

Kayla was relieved. She didn't know why he was so squeamish about the doctor. Maybe he was embarrassed about not having any money. She didn't realize that this boy was so trapped. Even when standing in a deserted alley, his nerves were high strung. Fear. That's nearly all it took to hold this boy captive for his whole life. Without steel bars or weapons of force to contain him. He walked beside a successful, smart woman dressed for the white-collar world, but no one would have guessed the incredible pit of slavery this young teenager was trapped within.

At lunch, they picked up right where they had left off, only erasing the fight that separated them. She didn't ask questions about the orphanage. He engaged the conversation between bites of his two twelve-inch Subway sandwiches. A few wet napkins helped clean him up and they enjoyed lunch as they sat in her car in the parking lot. Midway through his second sandwich, she carefully asked some questions.

"So, what happened today?"

"I lost, what do ya think?"

"Oh. Who were you fighting?"

"Some guy from the next town over."

"Where's Catch?"

"He's not feelin' so good." He looked out the rearview mirror.

"What's wrong? Has he been to the doctor? What are his symtoms?" Will kept on chewing quietly. She thought maybe the doctor thing was a problem. "Well, is he gonna be OK?"

"Sure, he will. It's Catch. He always bounces back. Just

a few bad nights."

"Oh."

Kayla wanted to flood him with questions. Where was he living? Why was he fighting? What was he so afraid of? Where was his family? When was the last time he had eaten a good meal? Was he in school? How did he get to this place? But she knew better than to pry again. Maybe one day the answers would arrive at her front doorstep. Maybe one day she would understand the boy who constantly mystified her.

"You got any plans for Thanksgiving?" she asked.

"Oh yeah, sure, me and the fam, we're gonna pig out on a turkey. It's a real nice shindig."

"Oh, that's nice," she said.

"You?"

"No, not really."

"Aww, gee, smooth way to invite yourself, right?" He said with a laugh.

"No, no, no! I mean, I've got plans. My parents always invite me for dinner, so I may do that." The awkwardness of their destitute Thanksgiving plans started to set in. Will checked the time and insisted on getting home.

"Let me take you there. It's only getting colder out there, and you don't need to be walking in your condition. I insist."

After her persistence, Will conceded and directed her to a disheveled neighborhood. The houses were small, single-story homes with underground basements. Built in the 1950s on small lots, each residence had a rugged appearance with cracked siding and chipped paint. Random lawn furniture or used car parts were strewn in the front yards.

Once within a decent walking distance, Will requested to get out.

"I'll walk from here. It's not far, I swear."

"I really don't mind, Will. Just let me drop you off."

"Please. You can stop the car and I'll get out, or I'll just jump out anyway." He cracked the car door open.

"OK, OK." She slowed the car down. He got out of the car and bent over looking through the window. With protective warning, he pointed in the opposite direction.

"Get outta here as fast as you can." She nodded and watched him walk down the street and take a right at the next stop sign. It wasn't possible to follow him without being noticed. So, she did what any rational woman would do. She followed him by foot. The left side of Will's face was messed up and he limped slightly with each step while holding his ribs. The walk home required such effort that he never looked back.

Will hobbled down the middle of the street toward a house with cracked white paint and faded green shutters. Patches of shingles were missing on the green roof. A cheap beach chair with neon colors sat on the front porch. The grass was brown, but the weeds were flourishing. Kayla stood at the end of a tall scraggly hedge and watched Will painfully walk slower and slower. She focused on the sound of his footsteps and didn't hear the racing trot that moved in her direction.

The blur of a teenage girl flew through one of the large holes in the hedge. Kayla fell backward with an involuntary cry of shock. She looked up to see a pale white girl with long dirty blonde hair that flopped in her eyes. The girl whirled around toward Kayla and whispered a quick "Sorry" before running toward Will. She wore a dingy white V-neck undershirt with bleached jeans that were ripped in several places. A tattoo of three money signs ($$$) was on the side of the girl's neck.

"Will!" The girl gasped as she reached the edge of the

yard.

"Hey C." Will winced after turning too quickly for his injuries to handle.

"Will, where have you been? I've been looking everywhere for you."

"Yes, Will, where have you been?" A voice badgered from within the house.

A silhouette darkened the front entrance behind a worn screen door. Before the mysterious person stepped out into the light, Kayla's cell phone vibrated in her pocket and she dashed to the car.

"Hello?"

"Yeah, hi, Kayla? This is Josh." A sense of relief calmed her as her tires screeched out of the neighborhood.

"Oh, hi."

"Are you OK? Was this a bad time to call?"

"Yeah, I mean no, this is fine."

# CHAPTER ◻ 8

>>>>>>>>>>>>>>>

"YOU'RE LATE." The dark voice grumbled at the two teenagers. It was the ringmaster from the weekly fights who created the looming shadow before them. Dark, sunken circles formed under his eyes as he looked down at Will. Trying to hide the pain with each step, Will walked in a slow, protective manner in front of Celia who had grown quiet when she realized the eavesdropper was waiting at the door.

"Not late." Will looked defiantly into the man's eyes.

"Yeah, we still got time!" Celia looked over Will's shoulder. The two orphans stepped into the dilapidated house. This was the only home they had ever known. To the left was a small sitting room with vintage green upholstered couches arranged in front of a 19-inch television set propped on yellow plastic crates. On the couches were two elementary age boys and a girl watching re-runs of "Charlie's Angels." It was a dark home with old floral bed sheets covering the windows that sent an orange hue across the wall.

"Where ya been, Will? Don't keep us waiting." Will

walked past his leader without a word, and Celia's head dropped knowing she had given cause for suspicion.

"Just out," Will replied.

"Don't mess with me, you little good for nothing! I own you, remember?" The man leapt in front of Will with uncontrollable rage that quieted the entire house.

"I had to walk it off. I don't like losing, Boss." The man narrowed his eyes and looked down his nose at the boy. With such bruises on his face, the man couldn't tell if Will was lying or not, so he stepped to the side.

"It's Father, you jerk. Don't make me beat it into you. I provide all this for you, and if you ain't careful, you'll be out on the streets. You're getting' old, Will, you better stay useful. We don't have room for dead weight 'round here."

"Yes, Father." Will walked passed him and Celia followed. The Father lustfully looked her up and down while his hand sensually caressed the curves between Celia's legs as she walked by. She swallowed hard and ignored this dirty touch.

"Same goes for you, Celia." She swatted his hand away. The Father rebounded and grabbed her neck.

"Maybe you need to take a look in the mirror again. Remember the day you got that tattoo? Everyone who sees it knows you belong to me. Don't forget it!"

"Yes, Father."

The Father returned to the couch and put his arm around the eleven-year-old girl that sat next to him.

"Don't be late, kids. Mother hates it when you're late!" No one in the house knew this man's name. All the children and teens called him "Father." Some were so young they didn't even question it. Others thought it was a sick ploy to make the man feel loved. Only the "Mother" knew why. Mother was in the master bedroom and wore a silky floral bathrobe over her jeans. She was surrounded by alcohol bottles and a large bag of chocolates as she sat glued to the afternoon soap operas. Her red hair with graying roots was greasy, and she had not showered in several days, which was better than many of the kids in the house. It could have been her drug addiction, poor diet, or an insecure inner competition with the young girls she exploited, but she had grown particularly skinny over the years. Her knees were knobby, her legs and arms were gangly. The features on her face were sunken, and her skin was discolored with sunspots. She was sure that extra layers of red polish on her toenails made her beautiful, so she had one of the young girls give a weekly pedicure. Mother wasn't much of a mother, and Father wasn't a father at all, but if the children never knew their names, then it kept the home a stronger prison.

In the fall season the sun was setting early. By five o'clock darkness fell over the mountain range. The children in the house hated the dark. By four-thirty in the afternoon, all children were to be lined up in the basement ready for the evening. With faces scrubbed, hair brushed, and evening attire on, they waited for their inspection. The older ones helped the younger ones so as to avoid an eruption from the Mother or Father. Screaming was normal in that house, but there was nearly nothing worse than any of the children being late.

Not only was the punishment one that left a horrid mark, but it was also in front of all the children. The humiliation set the victim in line, but it also further entrenched the others in vicious fear for their lives. In a cold climate, heat always seemed to be the form of punishment. A hot iron to the top of a child's hand, a splash of boiling hot water from the coffee pot in someone's lap, a curling iron that scorched the delicate nature of a girl's upper inner thigh, or the hot edge of a fireplace poker that branded to the calves of a young boy; all were dreadful memories that turned to living nightmares for the children.

Though being on time and ready for the night seemed to protect them from a brutal lashing, the reality was that Mother and Father were so volatile that the children were never truly safe. With children ranging from infant to late teens, there was always a fair amount of drama in the house. Mother could explode over the toddler's soiled diaper, or Father might overreact to a boy's pestering remarks or endless questions of "why." Even more frightful was when the need for a drug fix started to take over. Those moments were the most merciless of all.

"In line!" The Mother cracked a wooden cane against the doorframe. The children snapped into line from the tallest to shortest. Celia stood at the end of the line with Will beside her, and the stair steps of sixteen others filled the hallway. The youngest was a three-year-old girl with thick brown bangs and a bobbed haircut. She was the greatest beauty in the room, the crowning prize of the house. Her name was "May" because she arrived at the house in May. Her eyelashes were long and her round face had the radiance of a porcelain doll. Her slightly plump figure made her look like a magazine baby model.

"Where's Catch?" The Mother looked at Will and Celia.

"Sick, Mother." Will remained face forward.

"Sick? Doesn't that lousy kid know he's costing us money? Look at me, Mothers don't get sick days! Welcome to the real world, when you're sick, you work."

"Mother, he's very sick this time," Celia said with a soft voice and her eyes facing the floor. All was quiet as Mother and Father exchanged glances in front of the children.

"Best to keep the kings happy." The Father left the room to start the van.

"Well, if Catch ain't here to do his part, that's just more

jobs for you to do tonight to make up for him, eh?" Mother snapped her fingers at them with a nasty twinkle in her eye. "Load 'em up."

It was just a few minutes before the hour and the first drop-off had to be made by five. Father pulled the brown fifteen-passenger van up to the back driveway and all the kids moved quickly and quietly to load in the vehicle. Some of the younger ones held hands. Celia led the way. Once packed in tightly, the Father drove to a series of locations.

For years, the Mother and Father had simply worked out of the house. Child exploitation was often a crime committed at the hands of a family member or trusted friend who brought offenders right to the front doorstep. This house was no different. When the kids were infants, it worked smoothly to have men of all ages come to the house for services. One room featured toddlers. One room was the traditional pre-pubescent girl's nightmare. The basement had camping tents with little boys waiting inside. A nursery was held in the master bedroom.

Though the children were too young and fearful to understand it, they were forced to satisfy every vulgar request they were given. The boys shivered as they heard footsteps thumping down the basement stairs. The girls wiped up and greeted their next suitor.

No one suspected the calls of visitors to a domestic house, but it did limit the clientele. It wasn't likely that an upper class man ventured into the rugged neighborhood for a fix. By cutting a deal with other dark circles, the adult couple worked the kids for longer hours, and reached a broader customer base with a higher price point. This also gave the opportunity to bring more kids in the house, which was how the Green House had reached an all-time high of nineteen children living under the roof at one time. Now each night a routine drop-off was made.

Will sat in the back seat with six others beside him. His head throbbed, and his ribs ached with the cramped conditions. He wondered what Kayla was doing for Thanksgiving. He had completely forgotten about the holiday until she had brought it up. He pictured her eating turkey and pie, and he could not decide if he wanted to hate her for it, or if he simply longed to be there with her. He couldn't think of many things to be grateful for on this cold night. His best friend lay with cold sweats, convulsions, and bloody diarrhea back at the house with undeniable signs of a recently contracted STD. Celia was assigned to the most ferocious of all stops, and Will had recently transitioned to a new set of clientele. Mother had sprayed perfume in the car so all the children came out smelling nice, but the aroma only agitated his headache. The notion of gratitude was hardly in his vocabulary. While others around the city prepared for a holiday feast, these children were staring into the dark abyss outside the van. The children in this house quickly associated darkness with this dreadful ride.

Just as the Jews were promised freedom in exchange for working in Hitler's camps, a similar lie was promised to these little ones. Each night had a new list of drop-off points all over the city. Whether going to the back doors of strip clubs, bars, massage parlors, manicure salons, adult toy shops, XXX rated video stores, or just a house in a residential area, the children never knew where they would be left. Many times the Mother worked through an online ad on CraigsList or backpage.com. Photos of the children were posted all over the internet advertising their availability. House calls were often made to the outskirts of Denver. The pre-teen girls shuddered when they passed a truck stop on the highway. Those were some of the darkest, coldest corners to be assigned for the night. Countless truckers would drive nonstop and park in line to get their fifteen-minute fix.

Mother sat in the front seat with a list in her hands and when the van drew near the next stop she would turn and call out the child's name. The chosen one immediately moved to the sliding door of the van. Upon arrival, Mother rushed the child to the back door of the facility. With a knock on the metal door, she straightened the child's hair. She looked them in the eye and gave a sick motherly order.

"Now, be good for Mother. Don't let me hear that you've been bad. You do as you're told now. You hear? Do as you're told and they'll take good care of you." When the door opened, she pointed to the man standing before them. "This is your King. You do everything the King tells you, or you will wish you were dead."

Will watched with each stop as the children were whisked away with the promise of happiness and death all in the same breath.

They didn't wear a gold star on their sleeve, there was no law forbidding their existence, and there was no tyrant systematically destroying their entire culture. They were just kids. These were little children desperately clutching for dear life, with no voice to cry for help, and no one to stand up for them. Like the kids who had been packed into trains on cold German nights under the guise that their compliance might save them, these children were equally blinded by deception. Silence ruled over them. A child is born with a heart full of hope. Even when the night before was tragically abusive, a child could still believe the words of their Mother or Father that freedom was on the horizon. They believed that the next day could be better. They had endless hope that fairy tales would come true, and life would one day mirror the stories of their heroes. Even when all had been squeezed from them, and their tears stained the thin floor mats they slept on at night, a Mother's whisper would restore hope. They were children. Born to hope.

But Will was not a child any longer. Hope had died years ago, and a hard façade had covered his heart. Will was living in a constant state of survival mode. However, even though it seemed as though all hope was lost, and he had forgotten how to love out of sheer necessity, there was, in fact, still the tiniest spark of warmth deep within Will's soul. He couldn't see it. Mother and Father didn't know it was there, but Celia couldn't ignore it. Something in her gut told her to squash it, or douse it with a spoonful of reality for Will's best interest, but she just could not do it. She liked Will. She always had. In fact, she loved him.

Will and Celia were dropped off last. In the past, they had been rented out to the same location each night. Father had told Will to make sure Celia didn't end up dead. She had a free spirit and a bit of boldness in her words that could easily get her into trouble. Father knew that a girl with her looks could make it into her early thirties in this business if she survived. So, for the sake of longevity and his personal fortunes, Father had assigned Will to keep an eye on Celia. Unfortunately, though, things had changed in the recent months. Will was looking like less of a boy and more of a man. He was winning more fights; his body was lean and growing more muscular as each month passed. Under the advice of one of the "Kings," Will transferred to a new community of upscale clientele. Catch had been moved over to this scenario at a much younger age, and the wear on his body was noticeable. Now, as Will spent each night being raped for the fantasies of thirty or forty different men in the backroom of a night club, he feared that neither he nor Celia were very well protected anymore. Ever since his recent transfer, Celia had more "sick days", more bruises, and more unexpected callers arriving back at the house. Since the official shift to the drop-off strategy, and an increase in child prostitutes living in the house, all business had been kept off site. Still, despite the danger, Father had said that Celia was a big girl and could handle herself. In the dark of the night, Will watched as Celia walked herself up to the back door and entered upon "the King's" approval. The boy looked up and saw Father staring at him in the rear view mirror. With a wrinkle of defiance in his nose and a teenage effort at independence, Will uttered a sarcastic dig.

"Happy Thanksgiving." The Father looked forward and began the drive a few streets away. Will knew he would be arriving soon, so he had to toughen up and mentally prepare for the night's sex routine. If he didn't act like he enjoyed it, then he might not meet his quota of forty clients that night. No matter how the schedule panned out, after the Kings took their fee, Will had to bring home $1000 profit every night, six nights a week. If Will didn't produce the right income, Father would match him up in a fight like the one he had that day. He didn't like losing. Not one bit. So, like a Greek actor parading with a painted mask, Will shed the bits of humanity left in his soul, and stood up in the dark alley with a charade of confidence. He walked with his chin up and shoulders held back. Standing at the door he knocked three times and then twice more. As he waited, he wondered where Kayla was at that moment, but he had to break thought because the jealous image of her celebrating with the family was more than he could bear. He wiped Kayla from his mind and flashed a provocative smile as the rusted metal door opened.

# CHAPTER □ 9

>>>>>>>>>>>>>>>

WHEN Josh invited Kayla to attend a Thanksgiving service, she couldn't come up with a good excuse fast enough. Josh had a positive expectance in people that made it impossible to turn him down. So, Kayla stood in front of her closet with an arm full of clothes. She held a few blouses in front of her and looked in the mirror. She cocked her head and tapped one foot on the floor. Each outfit was tossed on top of Jack who was sound asleep on her bed. She shoved a few sweaters out of the way and rubbed Jack's ears as she stared back into the closet.

"What am I supposed to wear at a church? There's no way I am going to fit in. Why do I even care? Ya' know, I'm not going." She dug through the pile on the bed in search for her phone, and then paced the room as it rang.

"Hello?"

"Hi, Josh."

"Yeah, Kayla?"

"Yeah. Look, I'm sorry, I just don't think I can make it."

"Oh come on! It can't be that bad! Just pick something out to wear, we are pretty casual at church anyway."

"Oh, good. Wait, what? How did you--?"

"Kayla, you think I'm new at this? Everyone stresses over what to wear to church. I don't know why they make such a big deal about it, like God has a dress code or something? Seriously, I am wearing jeans and you'll probably make me look bad if you over dress."

"Really?"

"Really."

"OK, so I guess I'll see you tonight then."

Kayla smiled at the clothes strewn across the bed. *Was that a really lucky guess? Or is he right? Does everyone else stress about the same stuff I do?*

Josh was right. Church on the Rock was very casual. Many people dressed in sweaters and jeans, but it was not just the clothing that felt relaxed. As Kayla entered the lobby, she grew self-conscious, but the smiles around her were so genuine that she soon forgot about her worries. The worship center was different from the day before. Soft music played in the background and the atmosphere was warmly lit.

"I'm Dee Ann." Kayla hardly knew how to respond as the middle-aged woman with soft, feathery blonde hair gave her a tight hug. "I'm so glad you are here tonight." Kayla stepped to the side to avoid any conversation, but the woman followed her. *Do I know this woman? Or does she think I am someone else?* After a short chat, Kayla learned that Dee Ann was a woman with a huge heart and open arms. Kayla declined the invitation to sit with her, but appreciated the offer.

Kayla sat toward the back of the room and watched the service. The people sang songs, most of which she did not know. Some gave testimonies of their gratitude, and Josh gave a message that charged the congregation to look outside themselves and to give to others over the next few days. Overall, it was a pretty harmless experience. Not too preachy. No hell-fire and damnation saga. It was just people sharing life with one another. One person told a story about how he had not spoken to his son for over ten years and finally over the past week he made the effort to reconnect. With tears in his eyes, the old man gave thanks to God and pointed to his son in the third row who joined him that night. Kayla folded her hands in her lap thinking of her dad. She had told Will that she was having dinner with the family tomorrow. She wondered what might happen if she just showed up.

After the service, Kayla was not in the mood for mingling and it appeared that Josh was tending to the needs of others, so she tried to slip out the door before being noticed. Just as she reached the front glass doors, she felt a tug on her long black wool coat. The big blue eyes of a young girl were staring up at her. The girl couldn't have been much older than seven. Her porcelain skin and round pink cheeks were the perfect frame for a girlish smile. Loose blonde curls fell around her face and past her shoulders. She wore bright red corduroy pants, purple Converse All Stars, and a pale yellow top with white ruffled sleeves. Kayla's traditional feelings of distain crept up.

"Hi. Can I help you?"

"Hello. Are you Kayla?"

"Yes."

"Oh, good. Don't go," she said with a giggle. The girl pulled Kayla by the hand and led her back into the sanctuary. The crowd parted whenever this little girl ran by. The glances from the congregation made it seem as though she somehow belonged to all of them. Every few steps Kayla heard the loving whispers, "What's that Mattie up to?" "There goes Mattie."

"Mattie's found a new friend."

"Now sit here," Mattie said with a pointed finger. Kayla sat in the fourth row on the left side of the room and she watched as Mattie squeezed through the small group of people surrounding Josh. Though they were all engaged in conversation, once Josh felt Mattie tug on his belt buckle he immediately knelt down to hear her whispers in his ear. Josh looked up to see Kayla just a few rows away. He grinned and put one arm around Mattie. He pointed at the little girl as if surprised by her confidence.

"I see you found Mattie," he said with a smile.

"I think she found me, actually."

"Yeah, she has a way of spotting the newbies. She's a little preacher girl herself, always got a message stirring in her heart, and always looking to find new friends. I'm glad she found you."

"She was trying to escape, Dad!" Mattie jumped up from behind a row of chairs.

"No, I wasn't! I mean I--"

"Don't worry, you're probably not the first one to run from my preaching."

"Yeah right, Dad. You're the best!" Mattie held tightly to Josh's arm. He gave a bashful laugh. "He is! He really is!" She hopped at his side and giggled.

"Ok, sweetie. That's enough." Josh softly placed his hand on her shoulder.

For as cute as the little preacher girl was, Kayla was distracted and wondered what her own little baby Blanche would have looked like at that age. Consequently, this little girl, though adored by every other person in that room, put Kayla on edge.

"Hey Mattie, why don't you go check on Wade Bickerstaff and see if he ever found those cookies he was looking for. You know the hiding spot, right?" Mattie looked glum, but cookies were not a bad consolation prize.

"Aww, Dad, I can't show him the spot, then everyone will know!"

"Well, you'll just have to figure out how to share them without revealing your spot. I'm sure you can do it," Josh said encouraging his daughter. Mattie's eyes brightened as she sprinted off to fetch her cookies. The sanctuary started to empty out and Josh sat down backwards in the chair in front of Kayla.

"Glad you made it."

"So, you're a dad, huh?"

"Yeah, it's definitely the greatest assignment I've ever had." Kayla smiled at the way he seemed to relish in his role of fatherhood. She had never seen that side of her dad, but wondered how he might have responded if she had taken the time to ask.

"And you're a pastor?"

"Probably the hardest assignment I've ever had." His eyebrows raised and he smiled wide.

"Yeah, you didn't strike me as the preacher type."

"Really? What'd you take me for?"

"The janitor." Josh laughed out loud.

"Well, I guess a lot of pastors are kind of like that, ya' know? We're usually knee deep cleaning up someone's mess. Taking out the trash and cleaning toilets is the easy part."

"Yeah, I know what you mean. You probably deal with a lot of messes." Kayla gripped her journal and hoped the preacher could not see the mess she slopped around each day.

"Comes with the job, I guess."

"Well, I probably need to get going, got a long drive home, and work in the morning." The words slipped out so quickly that she hoped Josh didn't notice her courteous lie.

"Work? Tomorrow?"

"Oh yeah, ya' know. Big stories to write, stuff like that."

"Oh right, right, at the Post."

"Yeah, so I should probably get going." She stood and walked back to the lobby.

"Well, I hope you get a sliver of pie tomorrow. You can't have Thanksgiving without pie." Josh walked along with her. They were the last ones to leave and he flipped a few light switches off as they headed out the door.

"Mattie's a cute one. I wouldn't have thought she was yours."

"Wow, punch to the gut!" He mimicked a punch to his stomach with his own fist. Her cheeks turned flush.

"Oh crap, that's not what I meant. I just mean, she's got different features."

"Sure sure, try and recover from that one. Well, she's got the preacher gene from me, but her mama was truly beautiful. That's where the sparkle in her eyes came from."

"Well, she's real sweet."

"Thanks. I don't have any pie, but maybe I can wrestle one of those cookies from Mattie."

"Oh, no, I don't think I need to steal a kid's cookie. I'd have to do like 50 Hail Marys for that one, right?" Josh smiled as he walked to toward a closet door and waved for her to join him.

"Don't worry, we don't really do the Hail Mary thing around here. So, you're covered." He opened the closet and found Mattie with a boy her age sitting on the floor. Their cheeks were packed full of Oreos, and they clutched more cookies. Covered in crumbs, they looked up at him with delight. Mattie muttered a greeting through the mouthful of cookies. With hands in his pockets and eyebrows raised, Josh attempted a stern response, though the love for his daughter translated into muffled amusement.

"Well, hello, Mr. Bickerstaff. Mattie, I suppose you're gonna have to find a new hiding spot for your stash, eh?" Mattie mumbled another response that only Josh could interpret. Josh called over his shoulder, "Hey Dee, we're gonna need help locating Wade's parents. He may have overdosed on Oreos again." The sound of heeled footsteps echoed down the far hallway and Dee Ann emerged around the corner.

"I needed to get out of that office anyway," she said. Dee Ann bent down to the children's level, beckoned the young boy, and snatched a cookie for herself. "Ok, little man, off to find your mama. She's probably wondering what you're up to."

"I don't know what I'd do without Dee Ann," Josh said. "Not every assistant has Miracle Worker written on their resume." Dee Ann rolled her eyes and patted his back while walking out the front doors.

"He buys my loyalty with kind words and lots of strong coffee. So nice meeting you, Kayla. Hope to see more of you soon!"

The package of Oreos was nearly empty. Josh picked it up and shoved a whole cookie in his mouth then extended one toward Kayla. She accepted.

"So, you've got my cell. Call me if you ever need anything."

"Well, I am sure you probably have enough messes to deal with," she said waving the Oreo in his direction.

"Oh, I meant for your articles for the Post. But in that case, you're totally welcome, too. I'm always around. So, if you ever need anything. I'll be here, and I'll probably have cookies." He handed her another cookie, which she took and then waved goodbye to Mattie.

"Thanks for finding me, Mattie." The little lady grinned from ear to ear with her teeth completely covered in black crumbs.

Headed out into the chilly evening, Kayla looked up at the stars. On her way home, Kayla stopped and bought three packages of Oreos and a fresh gallon of milk. She sat on her couch surrounded by cookies and a large glass of milk. Kayla ate Oreos into the night and watched her favorite episodes from seasons four and five of *Friends*. Tonight she was happy, thankful. This week she had made friends. She even let Jack lick the inside cream of one or two cookies.

When Kayla woke up the next morning, she could still taste the sweet remnants from the night before. She stayed in her pajamas all morning after she opened the blinds to see an overcast day with a wet chill in the air. The smell of strong coffee filled the small apartment, and Kayla was happy to be greeted by the Macy's Day Parade on television. The music, floats, big balloons, and Rockettes all reminded her that this day was supposed to be something special. She had told Will that she was spending the holiday with her family, but she wondered if they wanted to see her. *What if they won't talk to me? What if it turns into a heated ordeal? Who wants that?* She convinced herself that they wanted nothing to do with her. She almost called her sister several times that morning, but put the phone down each time.

Kayla wanted to call, but she didn't. She wanted to smell her mother's turkey and gravy, but she settled for cold cereal that day. She wondered about Will. She wondered about Josh and his Mattie. She sat on the edge of her seat knowing that her dad and the rest of the family were most likely also watching the Broncos take a beating by Kansas City. She knew her dad was eating Mom's amazing Mexican layered queso dip with a bottomless bowl of chips. She hated when the Broncos lost, but it was worse cheering for her team alone. So, game after game, and season after season, she thought of her dad, and wished she could eat junk food with him on game days. Sometimes she even wore the jersey her dad had given her years back, just to pretend she wasn't alone.

That winter was an unforgettable one for Denver and all the surrounding Colorado cities. Blizzards came the week after Thanksgiving. Then again in early December. And again in mid-December. In addition to the stress of dirty snowdrifts, frigid temperatures, and constantly driving on ice, Kayla could not get to Will. One afternoon she left work and navigated the old neighborhood hoping to find Will's house. All the houses looked the same, and snow was piled high in the yards. After an hour of searching, she made her way back to the apartment.

Dec. 15, 2008

WHERE IS HE?!? So worried. Is he warm? Is he eating? Is Catch better? Why is this so hard? Maybe I should just leave him alone.

That night she dreamed again of the scene when she almost hit Will with her car. This time when he slammed his hands on the hood of her car Will looked up at her. Their eyes met. He smiled. Kayla woke up in the middle of the night and knew she had to find that boy. Each day she watched the weather. Her hope cried out from so deep within her that indeed, her hope had morphed into a desperate prayer.

Dec. 19, 2008

Snow again. But only 2-3 inches.

SO... I am going. Tomorrow. Please let me find him.

# CHAPTER □ 10

>>>>>>>>>>>>>

WITH a quick stop at Starbucks, Kayla bought two hot chocolates. White clouds had fallen again on the city, but no one seemed to care at this point. The jingle of holiday cheer was unmistakable as Christmas music was played on the radio. Storefronts glistened with fake trees, big bows, and wrapped presents. The streetlights were decorated with gingerbread men, candy canes, and holly leaves.

Kayla drove to Will's hidden boxing ring. Beside her on the floor of the passenger side of the car was a thermal lunchbox with hot soup and corn bread inside. Warm pumpkin muffins were wrapped in aluminum on the passenger seat, and an extra large bag held nearly three-dozen homemade chocolate chip cookies. Snow fell and she drowned out thoughts of fear with the iconic music of the season. Bing Crosby's "I'm Dreaming of a White Christmas" gave her hope that she would soon find this lost boy.

It was 29 degrees with two inches of snow on the ground, and Kayla saw businessmen walking with long coats and black leather gloves along the side of the street.

The fight moved to a basement in of one of the brick buildings. Old wooden doors were standing open, revealing a staircase filled with people. The men were not as loud this time. It might have been the cold air billowing in through the open doors, or the fact that the view of the fight was guarded and people were more focused to see who was winning. Kayla pulled her hat off and ducked behind the shoulders of the men, peeking over to see the action.

Will was fighting Catch again. His nose was bloody and, again, Catch favored his left ribs. A girl walked across the room wearing seductive clothing and took cash in each hand. The man who ran the bets utilized the persuasions of a beautiful assistant, the girl from Will's neighborhood. Kayla hid in the crowd along the back wall and caught a few glances of the fighters, but mostly read the body language and listened to the comments of the men around her.

Will lost. People left, and Kayla remained hidden while they filtered out. She waited until the leader left with his pockets full of cash. Walking down the steps, she watched as Catch brought Will's shirt over and wiped his friend's brow with it.

"Come on, man. It's getting nasty out there. Gotta get back to the house," Catch said. Will sat up, holding onto his knees propped up in his chest. He looked up and his eyes met Kayla. Just as she had dreamed, he smiled when he saw her. She smiled back. A side door to a small bathroom flung open and the assistant walked into the room. She wore bleached ripped jeans, sneakers, and a knitted sweater with extra long sleeves. A bag with her lacy outfit was hanging on her arm, and she was pulling pins out of her hair.

"You need something?" The girl stood with her hands on her hips and head cocked to the side.

"Just looking for Will," Kayla said. The girl looked over to see that both boys were smiling at the strange lady standing on the steps in front of them.

"Do I know you?"

"I don't think so. I am Kayla."

"Celia." Kayla's mouth dropped a bit and she looked back at Will as if she wasn't allowed to speak Celia's name. All she knew was that, to Will, this girl was special and to be protected.

Will walked Kayla back to her car where they retrieved the lunch. Back in the basement, Kayla made a picnic for Will, Catch, and Celia. Everything was eaten. Celia ate more than anybody. At times she tried to maintain good manners, but mostly just scarfed her food and ate more without asking. Once the food began to hit their bellies, personalities started to rise up. Catch was always cracking a joke. Celia laughed at anything the boys said. Will was more quiet, but thoughtful and attentive to the family sitting around him.

"It's pretty sweet of you, K-doll." Catch had a flirtatious smile and a sparkle in his eyes.

"I wanted to send cookies home with you, but I guess I should have brought more." Kayla folded the empty plastic bag.

"Yeah, well if we brought that stuff home, we'd never see it again," Catch said with an upbeat sarcasm as he stretched his arms and leaned back a bit. Both Celia and Will gave sharp disapproving looks with squinted eyes and pursed lips as though to muzzle him. "Well, I mean, with so many kids in the orphanage, they would all want some."

"What do you guys do for Christmas at the orphanage?" Catch looked stunned with wide eyes and an open mouth. He glanced to Celia and Will sitting at each side, but they dropped their heads and set their eyes between their knees. Now he had talked himself into a corner.

"Uh, well, ya know, the usual holiday stuff."

"Like what?"

"Sing songs and all that…"

"Do you guys have Santa come visit? Or get presents?"

"Maybe you missed the part where we said we was orphans. We don't have no mom, no dad, and last time I checked on how all that Christmas stuff works, that usually means no Santa either. Thanks, Kay, just rub in it a little more, eh? You got some salt for our wounds?" Catch was gaining skill and confidence in his story. Will and Celia smiled with amusement at the way their friend could turn the conversation around.

"Oh, I'm so sorry. Sometimes I get my nose stuck in places… and I don't, well, never mind. I'm sorry." Kayla bent over a bit and started nervously folding the empty cookie bag.

With eyebrows raised Catch rubbed his hands over the back of his head.

"It's ok. Don't worry. I don't have much, but what I have, I wouldn't trade. Who else gets to whip up on their best friend every week?" Catch playfully jabbed Will who looked up with a flare of competition in his eyes.

"Oh yeah? You're like one for ten. They call you Catch cause all you catch is my muscle in your face!" Will teased back as he attempted to lock Catch in a wrestling hold. The boys laughed and grunted with challenging words as they rolled around on the floor.

"You like that? Huh?"

"Bring it on."

"Come on, where's your muscle now?"

The boys rolled around on the dirty floor like toddlers surrounded by their toys. One pinned the other down for a second before the other escaped and leapt on top. Kayla smiled watching them. She could not help but notice that Celia shared the same endearing look for the boys.

With all the snow on the ground, Kayla insisted on driving them home. This time she made mental notes of every street name and ever turn. The neighborhood was covered with snow, which made it even harder to remember where she was, but she was not about to let this connection slip through her hands. The kids ran from the car all the way to the front door. Will was the last one up the steps. As the others rushed through the front door, he turned and looked back at her with a smile and slight nod of his head. This was the smile from Kayla's new dream. The smile that looked like it might warmly burst through his eyes. The smile communicated, "Thank you" and "I need you" all without ever saying a word. Her heart swelled, her throat tightened, and all she could do was wink and nod her head while holding firm control over her quivering lips. She loved him. She didn't know it yet, and she couldn't articulate her confused feelings, but love was growing in her heart again. In the car on the way back to work, Kayla's thoughts were flooded with ideas. The faces of her orphan friends were on her heart, and she wanted to do something special.

Kayla arrived home with a mission that day. Walking in the door, she headed straight for her closet. Reaching to the back of the closet, she pulled each hanger aside. Finally she found it. She sat on the bed with the jacket in her hands. Tears blurred her vision as heated memories came flickering back. Looking inside the jacket, the collar had been stitched with letters that read: G. Cole.

Gregg was the first and last boy she ever loved. She thought it was the forever kind of love, until she watched him drive away as she walked into the clinic that day. Weeks later as their relationship crumbled, Gregg didn't dare ask for his

Broncos jacket back. She had always kept it. Her anger burned every time she saw it, but something in her just couldn't throw it away. Now, as her fingers ran across the stitching above the tag, she sighed out loud in relief. It was finally time to let it go. Let him go. And a simple seam ripper would erase the name that had marked her for years.

"What are you doing here?" Josh spoke with a happy surprise in his tone. The worship service had just let out, and he had not expected to see her sitting in the crowd on that Christmas Eve Sunday morning.

"Well, thanks. Didn't they teach you how to welcome people in preacher's school?" She was never usually so confident. It was almost as if she had forgotten the history of the walls around her. But today she had a plan and her heart was lighter because of it.

"Merry Christmas, Miss Kayla!" Kayla stumbled as Mattie tackled her with a hug. Josh reached out to catch her but she regained control before their hands met. Kayla's heart still rose up with tension around the little girl. Her hand softly rubbed Mattie's blonde curly hair, but she soon took a step away as her stomach tightened. She knew in her head that this girl was precious and safe, but Kayla held her heart above Mattie's short reach. The little girl, though endearing, still scared Kayla, and reminded her of all that she was missing out on with her Blanche.

"Merry Christmas, to you, Mattie," Kayla said.

"I guess she has the greeting thing down a little better than I do," Josh said with a smile as he scooped Mattie up in his arms and planted her on his hip.

"Oh, I've missed you, girl!" Dee Ann whispered in the midst of a tight hug from behind. Kayla nodded as she felt the grip bring new strength.

"I just wanted to say thanks for everything. The canned food was a great idea. I think they will really like it," Kayla said as she turned back to Josh.

"Don't thank me, I am just glad the food pantry was well stocked when you called last week. That's what it's there for anyway."

"Well, thank you, still."

"Anytime. Did you drop everything off yet?" he asked.

"Not yet. I'm gonna grab some lunch and bring everything over this afternoon. Thought it would be fun to surprise them right before Christmas."

"Oh wait! There's one more thing to add to the pile!" Dee Ann rushed to the kitchen on the back side of the building.

Josh and Dee Ann both walked Kayla to the car with a twenty-five pound turkey in tote and gasped as she opened the trunk for a place to set it down.

"Woah! Look at you, Mrs. Claus!" Josh marveled and pointed at the different goodies in the trunk.

"I am just stunned. This is so awesome." Dee Ann clasped her hands together. Kayla couldn't help but think her efforts were rather meager despite their praise.

"Well, have fun," Josh said.

"And Merry Christmas," Dee Ann added.

"Thanks." Kayla spun the car keys in her hands.

"Yes, Merry Christmas," he said as he laid the turkey in trunk.

"You, too," she smiled as she shut the trunk door.

Kayla wanted to laugh out loud, stomp her feet, and dance. Anything to let the energy out. She drove like a teen-ager in love with fast turns and loud music. She hadn't slept the night before, all she could do was retrace the route and the roads leading to Will's house in her mind. It was nearly three o-clock and she couldn't wait to burst in the doors.

She left the trunk open, and held a laundry basket full of small wrapped Beanie Baby toys in her arms. These were a collection from her youth and she was excited to pull them out of her closet and share. She walked tall with light steps up to the front door and knocked loud.

"Hey Catch. Is Will here?" Catch peeked through a crack in the door. He didn't seem himself. His eyes were blood-shot; he looked like he had just gotten out of bed. When he turned to yell for Will, she noticed how his posture slumped and his head hung. Will arrived looking equally ragged, and his gaze kept looking out over her shoulder as though he was awaiting someone else's arrival.

"I've come with a surprise!"

"Huh? What for?"

"For Christmas, of course!" She gestured to the laundry basket full of presents. Will hesitated and brushed the hair out of his face with his hand. Kayla's insecurities seeped out and she started to worry. She bit the side of her lip, and stared down at Will's knees, but then noticed a smaller hand take hold of the door. Two beautiful brown eyes peeked around. Kayla was given hope at the sight of a cute little nose, and then finally, a tiny smile.

"Hi, there. What's your name?" Kayla bent down to her

knees and looked the little girl in the eyes.

"Get back, May!" Will scolded the toddler with a shove. May's face disappeared, but Kayla could still see her hands holding tightly to the door.

"Hi, May, did you want some Christmas presents? I have so many presents here, and I just want to share them with you all." Kayla heard a faint little voice from the other side of the door.

"Really?"

"Yes, ma'am."

"Yeah! Guys! Guys! Presents!" Little feet thumped as May jumped behind the door. Kayla looked up at Will and saw his gentle smile.

"I'm gonna need your help carrying this stuff in." Kayla pointed to the open trunk behind her. It took Will, Kayla, Celia, and Catch to carry in the carload of gifts. All the other kids waited with anticipation inside the front door as the parade of presents began. Catch held the turkey over his head and bellowed a jolly "Ho, Ho, Ho!" The gifts were spread out across the family room and the children cheered over every single one. First Kayla had a large box full of canned goods and non-perishable products. The children passed each around and Kayla was touched by the expression of wonder over canned corn and potatoes. Then Celia passed out the small gifts for each child. They tore into the wrapping paper and celebrated the brightly colored plush toys. May hugged a teal hippo in her arms. She squeezed him, danced, twirled, and taught him the tango in a constant burst of joy. When Kayla unveiled the box of freshly baked cookies, she laughed as they dove with open hands for the treats. Catch, Will, and Celia enjoyed the moment of giving just as much as Kayla.

"Good thing I made four batches! Though, I'm not sure

if these will last till morning." The crowning moment came when one of the boys pointed to a gift sitting behind Kayla. This boy had remained withdrawn and sat on the couch during the party. He didn't maintain eye contact with anyone, and he never spoke. He flinched when she moved toward him. She held her distance, and pointed at the gift.

"Open up and see," Kayla slid the box toward him. The boy slowly ripped the wrapping paper. With a silent gasp he hugged the gift and placed his cheeks on the box. Another boy noticed the gift and jumped for joy.

"Wii! Wii! I don't believe it! Look!" The kids didn't catch on, until the boy turned and showed them the box. "It's a Nintendo Wii! This is the best day of my life!" The children cheered. Will, Catch, and Celia sat with mouths open in pure amazement.

"Seriously?!" Catch picked up the box and pulled out the game pieces. The other children jumped around him with their hands in the air as they reached for the new game.

"I thought a house full of kids could really have some fun with it," Kayla said. It only took about five minutes to break into the box and set up the new game system. The older kids chaperoned and kept the younger ones in line for their turn to play. Kayla sat on the floor and enjoyed the Christmas moment. She soaked in the atmosphere of the small, run down house. The furniture was probably forty years old and sat low to the floor. The edges of the seat cushions were frayed, and a layer of grime covered nearly everything in the house. She noticed a piece of metal décor hanging crooked on the wall that almost looked like a license place. Imprinted on the metal were the words "Green House."

"You better get going. The old man will be home soon, and the presents are real nice, but he don't like visitors much."

Will spoke in a hushed tone. Kayla kept her eyes fixed on the metal plaque.

"What's that? Is that his name? Green?"

"Uh, yeah. Green," he said. "Like I said, time to get going." Will gently slipped his hand in her arm and started to pull her toward the front of the house. He opened the door, and the cold air rushed in which reminded Kayla of her last present.

"Oh wait! Come here! One more thing!" Kayla ran out to the car and pulled a wrapped present from the back seat. Will folded his arms tightly, bracing himself from the cold in short sleeves while standing on the porch. "This is for you," she said. Will cocked his head and gave a little side smile. He sat down on the top step, suddenly numb to the cold, and focused on the gift in his lap. She could hear the muffled sounds of the children playing with their Nintendo Wii and stuffed animals inside. "What's wrong?" She watched him stare at the brightly colored wrapping paper.

"I kinda like the way it looks just like this."

"Oh come on! You gotta open it. The faster you open it, the faster you can use it."

"Yeah, but it's almost more fun to just wonder what's inside."

"Come on, now! I am gonna open this for you, if you don't!" She shook the present and squealed with excitement. Will smiled back up at her and ripped the paper. His eyes lit up when he saw the dark blue jacket. Without hesitation she flung the jacket over his shoulders. A perfect fit. She never would have thought that holding on to Gregg Cole's hand-me-down jacket could be so rewarding.

"This is... just... unreal!" Will raised his arms and cheered with half a laugh. Kayla grinned watching Will strut on the steps with his new jacket.

"Well, I gotta keep you warm."

"Yeah, but it's the Broncos. It's my team!" Will looked down at himself stroking the jacket.

"You like it?"

"I love it!" Will grabbed her tightly and pulled Kayla in for a huge hug. She felt his skinny ribs underneath her arms. He was still nearly her height but it would only be a few months before he was taller than she was. She smiled at his response, and as she looked over his shoulder, she saw Catch smiling in the front window. Catch's nose crinkled with a smile and he gave a thumbs-up.

"Will." Celia spoke softly as she stepped in the doorway.

"Isn't this awesome?" He turned toward her and held out the zippered edges of his jacket.

"It's perfect," she said with a smile. Kayla could see that Celia loved Will like a brother just as much as she did. Celia's eyes were delicate and concerned for both Catch and Will. "But it's almost four o'clock. She's gotta go quick." Celia held the empty laundry basket and pushed it out on the front porch while shivering from the cold air. Will looked back at Kayla with a childlike smile.

"This is the best. Thank you, thank you!"

"It's nothing."

"No, this is awesome."

"Will, come on." He glanced back to see Celia's pleading eyes.

"Yeah, OK," he said in her direction. Looking back at Kayla he put his arms on her shoulders. "You gotta go. The old man will be back, and we gotta clean things up before he comes."

"Sure, no problem," Kayla walked back to the car with her basket in hand. Will followed her. "Maybe I can see you around New Year's? Sometime after Christmas?"

"Definitely," he said with a smile.

"Merry Christmas," she said as she started the car.

"Merry Christmas." While leaving the Green House, she drove off and watched him in the rear view mirror. She noticed that he didn't shiver with his arms held tightly, or shuffle his feet out of cold nervous energy. He was warm, and that made her happy.

Nothing could have topped that Christmas Eve, but she feared that her next stop would douse it all. Driving to a familiar place from her past still felt natural. It wasn't until she pulled into her parents' subdivision that she gripped the steering wheel tighter and her back arched with tension. Filled with anxiety, Kayla actually passed the house twice. Finally on the third time approaching the house, she turned into the driveway.

Kayla took a few deep breaths, straightened her outfit, and rang the doorbell. A young teenage girl answered the door, and Kayla's stomach dropped.

"Hi, Rudy," Kayla said with quivering nervousness. She scratched her forehead and took a few deep breaths. Rudy looked at her aunt as though she were a stranger.

"I'm Kayla. Your mom's sister…"

"Mom, Kayla's here." The teenager shouted into the house, turned back and left the door open while heading back to the kitchen. Kayla took a step closer. Her mouth watered as the smell of her mother's turkey stuffing floated to the front door. Looking down at the hard wood floors and the worn front entry rug, Kayla heard the thumping of footsteps come down the stairs.

"Hey, Kat," Rex said with a smile. Kayla didn't cringe at the nickname, she actually liked it this time. His eyes had soft wrinkles around the edge which were now wet with tears. Before she could say anything, her daddy wrapped his arms around her in a tight hug. They stood embracing one another, and she exhaled into his shirt. Still biting her lip she tried desperately not to sob. He held her and whispered in her ear.

"It's been too long, baby girl. Too long."

She nodded her head, buried in his chest. Warm tears dampened her daddy's shirt. The two stood there for a timeless moment, making up for the years lost, the Christmases past, and silently forgiving each other for all the harsh words said.

That evening Kayla felt as though she tiptoed back into the family life. She watched everyone interact. At first she felt awkward, and did not know how to catch up on over a decade of life. Her dad made a point to include her in conversations. Everyone was there. Rachel and Ryan now had three kids. Her brothers laughed and teased one another throughout the evening. Regina's cooking was even better than Kayla had remembered. Rex had softened over the years. His face had relaxed with a few wrinkles and creases. His eyes and gentle touch revealed how much more Rex appreciated his family. Kayla figured it happened over the years as he watched his grandchildren grow. But the truth was that Rex's heart broke when Kayla left, and as it mended over time, he realized that family was more important than his job or the public opinion.

The smells of cinnamon, sweet potatoes, juicy turkey, and the fresh live Christmas tree all bonded the family in the glow of twinkling lights and Christmas jazz music. The family went to church. They ate dinner, and raved about Kayla's homemade pumpkin pie and pumpkin cobbler. There was not a hint of awkward tension or grudges from the past. Kayla hugged her mom and shared recipes. The whole family piled in the living room to watch *Home Alone.* The children laughed, but the adults laughed even harder as they enjoyed the movie with nostalgic memories from their own childhood.

"Remember when Ricky tried to sled down the stairs like Kevin?"

"Or how about when Robby tried cutting down his own Christmas tree, and chose Mom's favorite tree in the front yard?" All of the siblings were squished on the couches, and Kayla's little brother, Ricky, put his arm around Kayla as they enjoyed the holiday movie. She didn't want to be anywhere else.

It was late, and at her mother's urging, she stayed the night in her old room. The sheets smelled clean, and nothing about the room had changed since she left for college. Stuffed animals lined the bed, and faded posters were still pinned to the wall. Her mother sat on the bed beside her and tucked her in. Regina's soft fingertips caressed her daughter's cheeks.

"Merry Christmas, baby girl."

Dec. 24, 2008

Wow. Unexpected wonderful. Had dinner with the family. Where have I been all these years? Just glad to be home. So glad.

# CHAPTER ❑ 11

WHEN the Mother and Father returned to the Green House, they were shocked to find the children playing with the Nintendo Wii and stuffed toys.

"What's all this?" The Father had an added growl in his voice. He bent over, and grabbed the toys from the children.

"It's Christmas!" May threw her arms in the air and jumped up and down with her hippo in hand.

"Not here, it ain't." Mother kicked the wrapping paper on the floor. "You gotta earn your keep. Get dressed! You got fifteen minutes, and better not be late or we are pulling the belt out real quick." The children's smiles faded, and Father noticed Will sitting on the couch wearing his new Broncos jacket.

"Hey, Elway, where'd this stuff come from?" Will looked in his lap without a word. "Look at me, son!"

"I'm not your son!"

"That's right, you're a worthless idiot with no future. I'd shoot you if you were my son. You're a waste. Just be happy I keep you around. You're gonna have to pay for that jacket.

111

Don't think I'm gonna let you steal from me!"

"I didn't steal it! It was a gift. Free!"

"Lie to me again, and I will rip your tongue straight out!"

"Wait, wait! He's not lying. This stuff was all free." Catch stood between them.

"Where? Who? Nobody cares about you guys. What makes you think I should believe that?" The children stood frozen, paralyzed by Father's thunderous yelling.

"Red Cross. Just some random, nice people with nothing better to do. Came to the door. Gave us this stuff. That's it. Nothing else." The children stood still and admired Catch's bravery. He always had the words to redirect the Father or Mother's attention. Father scratched his belly and nodded his head slowly. He still kept an intense stare on Will with his new jacket.

"You're still earning that tonight. You're working double time for that jacket." The Father grumbled orders in a low voice.

"Father." May tugged lightly on his pant leg and spoke in a meek voice. "Is Santa coming tonight?"

"Maybe, if you're good for all your friends tonight." The Father maintained his stare at Will. "It's Christmas Eve, ya know. Prime time for business." May looked down with disappointment.

"But, I don't like them, Father." Her eyes welled with tears. "I don't like it." Her little voice trembled. The Father bent down to her level, put his hands on her shoulders, and without a hint of compassion, berated the little girl.

"Don't you love your Father?" She immediately nodded. "I think you don't love me. Everyone knows you are ugly and these are the only people who want to give you love." The Father's threat grew intense as his voice quietly strained and teeth clenched. His eyes bulged with wild ferocity that terrified the little girl all the more. "So, you *will* take it, you hear. You *will* smile, and you *will* like it. If you don't smile, I might not be able to protect you. This is your life. This is all you get. Nobody will ever love you like I love you. So, you will do exactly what I tell you." His eyes softened with a lustful look toward the little girl. He brought his hand up toward her face, and May flinched as he caressed her dark brown hair. Tears rolled delicately down her round cheeks. Her pink bottom lip rolled out with instinctive sorrow, but she stood tall and strong without a word. His hand pulled her head over and he kissed the side of her neck.

When the Father stood up to face Will, he tightened every muscle, and stuck his chest out with his shoulders confidently held back. His raw, dry knuckles turned white with tightly gripped fists at his side. Like a wild dog challenging another with his eyes, the Father drew his chin down and his gaze bore into Will's stare, but Will would not let the tyrant in. Will's eyes were equally intense. He had grown stronger and taller over the past year. He didn't know any life other than this. He believed he was worthless. He believed that no one wanted him or cared for his existence. He thought he was dumb, and though he was growing into a man, he feared the dangerous network of traffickers in the Denver area. Running away was not an option. Freedom was a mocking fantasy. If Father didn't kill him, someone else would, and then who would watch over Celia or little May or the other small ones? He was trapped, and he had no idea how to get out. He didn't even know to dream of such things.

"Fifteen minutes! Line up in fifteen minutes!" The Father's voice shook the walls and the hearts of all the children. Still, Will did not move as the Father continued to stare him down. Little feet thumped up and down the stairs. The Father took a step toward Will.

"I said…"

"I heard you," Will raised his voice and turned his back on the Father and started for his room. With untamed force, the Father kicked Will on the underside of his butt which sent Will flying across the room where he landed on all fours. Burning pain flashed through Will's entire body. He gasped and grunted in desperation to breathe. He choked back tears and laid his head on the floor. The Father leaned down, grabbed Will's hair and viciously whispered into his ear. His words were vengeful, slowly separated, and Will shuddered as the Father's slobbery mouth touched his ear with each syllable.

"You think you're strong? Don't challenge me, kid. You will lose!" The Father stood up and kicked Will in the stomach, sending Will into the fetal position, gasping and moaning.

"Merry Christmas." The Father grabbed a beer and sat in the back yard. Will lay on the floor a few minutes until Catch came and hoisted him up.

"Can't be late, man. He'll kill you if you're late tonight."

"I wish he would just kill me and get it over with," Catch looked his friend in the eyes and Will thought better of his flippant comment. They needed one another. And they both knew it.

The week after Christmas welcomed a blizzard that shut down the whole city. The drifts piled fifteen feet high. The quiet days gave Kayla a lot of time to think. She pictured the ramshackle of a house that all of the orphans lived in. She imagined Will's face as he opened his only Christmas gift. The image of the Green House plaque was branded on her heart. She wanted better for Will, but she didn't know what to do.

"Something has to change," she said two weeks later. Kayla sat across the table from Will at their favorite Subway. Will wore his Broncos jacket and had a mouthful of chips.

"Huh?"

"Something has to change."

"What are you talking about?"

"You have to stop fighting."

"What do you mean?" Will swallowed his food and defensively sat tall in his seat.

"You are a kid. You should be in school, not fighting on the streets."

"I go to school!"

"Really?" Kayla said with her brow raised.

"Yeah, yeah. Homeschool. Me and the others, we do home school. Remember?" Kayla slouched down in her seat and looked at the ceiling while sipping her drink. Her mind raced as she tried to figure out how she could get Will out of the fighting scene.

"Will, you deserve so much more than this," she said still looking upward. Will leaned in with interest.

"Like what?"

"You're a smart kid, Will. You have inner strength. Maybe no one else sees it, but I do. There is something wonderful inside you just waiting to get out, ya know?"

Will sat on the edge of his seat, soaking in every word. No one had ever spoken that way about him. No one had ever dreamed up other possibilities.

"This fighting thing, it's not good for you. I worry about you. It's not safe. You are worth so much more." She had his undivided attention. "It's gotta stop." He looked away, and nervously popped his knuckles. Tension grew in his jaw. She sat forward, and put her hand on his hands. "Will, it's gotta stop." He looked down at their hands together. "Maybe I can help you. Maybe I can tutor you. I love English, I could help you with your school work." He was still silent. "Look, I'll make you a deal. What do you make off a fight each week?" He looked up at her, full of fear mixed with a twinge of hope. He was listening. "Three bucks, right? Well, I will give you ten dollars each week if you will stop fighting. And we can meet for lunch and work on your homework."

Will was stunned. Ten dollars was a lot of money for him, and it was money the Father and Mother would never know about. Kayla's ideas sounded good, but he couldn't imagine them actually becoming a reality. He pulled away from Kayla and shifted positions. A door of opportunity was opening, though he remembered the Father's threats. He didn't want Kayla to go away, but he also didn't want her to get hurt if she got too close. Propped up on his elbow, his hair fell across his eyes.

"I'll do it."

She burst into a huge smile.

"Really?"

"Yeah. Maybe you're right. Maybe there's more than this." Kayla laughed with excitement. Will didn't know how it would work, but his subdued half smile was all Kayla needed to see. Before leaving that day, she laid a ten-dollar bill on the table in front of him.

For months, Kayla diligently met with Will. They met

on Thursdays since he said that there were tests to be taken on Friday. Each week she came with an eager desire to watch him grow. The reality was that Will could not possibly quit fighting. The Father was not willing to sacrifice a fighter or his profits, especially if it was simply for the wellbeing of the child. So, Will had to fight smarter. He exercised in the early mornings in his room while the house was still asleep. He stole away to city parks to jog or do pull-ups or other exercises he couldn't get done in the house. When he stepped into his boxing ring, his focus was unmatched. He never took a hit in the face and never lost again. One time the fight was set for Will's opponent to win, but he didn't give in. The Father lost a lot of money that day and was furious. Will took a harsh beating and had to skip his weekly meeting with Kayla to recover, but he made it clear to the Father that he wasn't going to lose anymore. When the Father figured this out, he just set Will up against bigger opponents. And he still won. He didn't want a mark or trace of evidence to tip Kayla off that he might be fighting. Every time he fought, it was for her.

Schoolwork was the bigger challenge. He had Celia help him create tests or homework to show his tutor. Kayla assigned additional homework. She checked out books from the library for his summer reading and gave him small writing assignments. She helped him with better vocabulary and grammar. Months later, his frustration grew because he didn't naturally excel in his schoolwork as he did with his physical training. Considering he could hardly read to start with, he should have been pleased with his progress, but the stress of his schedule by day and by night was difficult for him to manage. Nonetheless, he kept trying. Kayla believed in him. She was the only person who did, and he didn't want to lose that.

"Did you get it?" When Kayla saw Evan walk out the elevator door into the newsroom, she skipped in his direction. Every few steps she slowed down to a walk, but excitement took over. The boy who had once been her greatest annoyance at work was actually coming through on a miracle. Evan stood tall with his chin raised and a teasing smile. He kept walking toward his cubicle and she followed back to their desks.

"Well? Did you get it?"

"Kayla, have I ever let you down?"

"Yes, actually. Lots of times. Remember when Stawlings about hung me out to dry over that disastrous story about the county commissioner, and you just sat there and…"

"OK, OK, bad question, never mind!" Evan reached into his jacket pocket and pulled out two tickets. "Well, this is your lucky day." He dangled them in front of her. Kayla grabbed the tickets and waved them around with a girlish squeal.

"Oh, I love you! I love you!" Kayla kissed the tickets. "You're the best!"

The rest of the morning Kayla could hardly focus. All she wanted to do was stare at the two Broncos tickets, which were now clipped to her computer screen. Evan's parents had season tickets and were out of town the upcoming weekend. After over a year of working together, Kayla knew more than she wanted to know about Evan's family Broncos obsession. They had Broncos wallpaper in the bathroom. Their dog's name was Elway. The kitchen had dark blue walls and orange plates. For as much as she loved the Broncos, Evan's family would have called her a fair-weather fan. Yet, they were an invaluable connection, and since they didn't need the tickets, they let her buy them for dirt-cheap.

Will wore his Broncos jacket every day for months on end and she was sure there could be no greater gift than to take him to the Mile High stadium in mid October. When she saw Will that day, she hopped up and down with the white envelope in her hands. He smirked at her silly behavior.

"Betcha want to know what I have!" She taunted him like a little sister.

"What?" He reached for the envelope. She drew it away and waved it in the air.

"Guess, guess, guess!" She held the envelope on her forehead like a mind-reader.

"You're crazy!" He said with a laugh. She pulled out the first Broncos ticket.

"Crazy, or not, I don't care. I am going to see the Broncos on Sunday!" Will's eyes lit up.

"Really? That's awesome." He was genuinely happy for her.

"Yeah, and you're coming with me!" She pulled out the other ticket. Will's mouth dropped but then turned into a huge grin as she placed the ticket in his hands.

"No way! Are you serious?" Will's eyes got larger and he started blinking in disbelief at the tickets.

"Forty-five yard line, baby! Fifteen rows up!" Will leaned his head back, looked up at the sky and cheered.

The rest of the tutoring session was sporadically interrupted by talk of the upcoming game, the players, and the overwhelming sense of gratitude. Will couldn't wait, but as Kayla taught him the difference between clauses and phrases, he realized that one barrier faced him. His whole nightlife. How could he get away? He would have to play sick, and it would have to be convincing.

"So, I'll see you Sunday? The game starts at 8:15pm."

"Can you pick me up at my house?"

"Sure. You wanna get there early? What time should I pick you up?"

"Yeah, let's say 6:15. And you hold my ticket for me. It's safe in your hands."

"Sounds good. I'll be there," she said.

That night Catch and Will devised a plan to fool the Mother and the Father. It had to be a gradual progression. On Friday night, Will acted sick with damp clothes making him appear feverish with chills and a pathetic cough. When looking him over, the Mother and Father weren't sure what to do. Catch suggested Will stay home, but Will said he was strong enough to make it through the night. The adults were happy to see Will's dedication, and this primed them up for the second night. On Saturday, Catch had collected as much dog poop as he could find, bagged it and brought it home. At about 4:00pm they loaded the toilet bowl with the foul smelling pile, and Will moaned as he sat on the seat. Red food dye in the toilet bowl made the scene even more convincing. This time the Mother suggested that Will stay home. The Father just stared at Will and loathed the prospect of losing a payout for the night. But again Will assured them that he could go out that night and earn his keep. This time, the Father was impressed by Will's determination.

Sunday was the crowning moment. Will and Catch had cleaned out leftover foods from the dumpsters of a few different restaurants. The afternoon began with the same diarrhea charade as the day before, this time not as severe. Then at about four o'clock, Will locked himself in the bathroom and pretended to be puking his guts out. When the Father started banging on the door, Will slipped an Alka Seltzer in his mouth to add some foaming action. He lay on the floor giving the performance of his life for the Mother and Father. The stench of food and feces made the bathroom nearly unbearable. The other children crowded around outside the door in the hallway. Catch didn't say a word. This had to be the Father's call. Will panted and laid his head on the toilet seat.

"I can go. I just don't want a beating." Will whispered with a sweaty pale face, and drool dripping from his mouth. The Mother looked at the Father with one eyebrow raised. "I'm fine. Be ready in a minute," he said. Then for the final act, Will's eyes bulged and he curled up over the toilet and began heaving uncontrollably.

"You're not going," Father said. The children were silent. Will moaned. "You puke like that on a customer, and we'll all be cut out of the circle." The Father left and slapped the doorframe. "Stay here." The children moved aside so the he could walk past them. Mother stood for a moment and watched as Will laid back down on the ground. Any real mother would have sat with him the whole night, washed his face, brushed his hair, made him soup. But she wasn't a mother at all. All she could think about was her heroin-fix that night, and that Will wouldn't help pay for it.

"What good are you? Clean up while we're gone," she said.

Will hated staying home knowing where Catch, Celia, and the others were headed that night. He watched out the window as the van drove off. When they were out of sight, Will jumped as high as he could and smacked the low ceiling with his hand. Father and Mother would be out all night shooting up, even when they knew he was sick. He gave the bathroom a deep cleaning, and took a hot shower. He hummed as he brushed his hair and pulled out the one clean shirt left in his pile. He set up his bed to look messy as though he had been sleeping in it, and pulled out a ratty blanket that was frayed and thin to put on top of the bed. Will waited at the door for nearly thirty minutes. For short moments he feared that Kayla might have given the ticket to someone else. He wondered if she remembered the way to the house. He let out a deep breath when her car turned the corner. She had hardly reached the driveway by the time he ran out the door and jumped in the car.

It was a perfect night. The Pittsburgh Steelers met the Broncos for a tough game, and 77,000 fans packed the stadium. It was loud. It was bleeding of energy and dramatic competition. Both teams had a few losses under their belts and both wanted the win. At thirty seven degrees, the truest fans were on their feet screaming into the night. The Steelers tied it up at the end of the fourth. It was an epic moment for everyone as the kicker, Jason Elam, nailed the game-winning forty-nine yard field goal. Bronco fans all across the stadium went nuts as their team won it out at 31-28. Kayla and Will soaked up every single moment of it. They shouted for Cutter and Crowder. They danced during half time. They ate bratwursts, and soda, and all the junk they could.

"This was the best night of my whole life," Will said as he stepped out of the car. It was just past one o-clock in the morning, and the house was dark just as they had left it.

"I am so glad." Kayla smiled. She tapped her fingers on the steering wheel.

"Thanks, Kay."

"We'll have to do it again sometime," she said.

"Sounds good." Will walked up to the lonely house.

October 21, 2009

Best night EVER!! Broncos won, but even if they didn't, I don't think I would have really cared. Seeing Will's face when he walked into the stadium was priceless. His mouth dropped and he looked up and up and up at the enormity of Mile High. Like a little kid in awe of the Christmas tree when it is first lit up for the season. I am sure I once was in awe like that years ago, but to get to see it in his eyes, in his face. It was like he was really safe. Really free.

# CHAPTER □ 12

>>>>>>>>>>>>>

"HOW did it go?" Josh asked. Kayla had been coming to the Wednesday night services at Church on the Rock off and on since the late summer. So far, no one had been mean to her, and it wasn't killing her, and it always encouraged her to see Josh and Mattie. The worship was a lot more contemporary then her traditional upbringing, but she was starting to like it a little. Wednesday nights after the service had become a time for Josh and Kayla to catch up. Sometimes she would pour out stories about Will, or she might have questions about church or other random issues. Dee Ann worked at her desk, while Josh and Kayla chatted in his office with the door open. The secretary brewed a fresh pot of coffee with smells that ushered in great conversations and questions. Mattie always had cookies, and one time Kayla brought a homemade chocolate chip oatmeal batch to share. On this particular night, Dee Ann couldn't help but jump on the love seat beside Kayla with excitement as well.

"Amazing. So amazing!" Kayla began with wide eyes

and big hand gestures. Her mind was moving too fast for her brain, and all she could do was spit out enthusiastic sentence fragments to describe her night at the Broncos game with Will. "He loved it. He was so in awe!"

"And they won, too, which never hurts," Josh said.

"Yeah, especially this season. I, honestly, didn't know what to expect, but it was an awesome game, awesome night. Will had the best time. When I dropped him off at home, he said it was the best night of his whole life. Can you believe that?"

"Wow. I don't know if I want to believe it." Josh folded his arms under his chest and took in a deep breath. Dee Ann already had tears welling up in her eyes.

"That's exactly how I felt." Kayla leaned forward and fidgeted with her fingers. "And that whole night, I couldn't sleep. Didn't know what to do. Just thought about him. Then I thought about how there are so many more kids like him out there. Orphans. Lonely, and no home. And I hate that."

"Me, too," Josh's eyes focused downward.

"So, I started writing." Josh looked up at her. "Just a lot of loose thoughts. My impressions of Will, my view of his world. Jotted things that I have done in recent months that seemed to impact him in some way. And I started thinking that maybe things might change if people knew about it, and they got involved, too. I want to research it more, like the whole process for adoption. I don't know. Maybe nothing will change… but then, maybe it will."

Kayla bit her lip having pitched her dream to Josh and Dee Ann. He rubbed the side of his cheek and processed everything she had shared.

"What do you think?" she said.

"I think you're right. Not for the sake of success, or promotion, but for people. Something in you is changing, Kayla, and whatever it is, it will take you where you need to go, and give you a fire to drive you to the end."

Kayla smiled, and braced herself as she heard little footsteps running in her direction. Mattie took a flying leap landing on both the women's laps. Josh's affirmation energized Kayla, and she took it out on his daughter with a good tickling war that left the little girl kicking and begging for more.

Pete Rivers leaned back in his swivel chair with the papers in front of him held high in the air. Kayla fidgeted with the pen in her hands as she silently stood waiting for Pete's feedback on her article.

"I like it." He dropped the papers down on the desk. Kayla waited for more remarks. Pete folded his arms over his belly, threw his reading glasses on the desk, and stared back at Kayla for a moment. "Did you hear me? I like it. Print."

Kayla could hardly believe what she was hearing. She broke a smile, which soon turned to a wide grin.

"Really? Is there anything we need to change? Too many words? Too poetic?"

"Print," he said with a smile. "Good, Barrington. It's good." Pete smiled back while handing the papers back to her. "Oh yeah, and one more thing. The "Colorado Writes" contest deadline is in three days. So get this to editing right now, and then get your stuff in by the first of November. This orphans thing, very compelling, and the world needs to hear this."

"Yes, sir." Kayla was beside herself. "Colorado Writes" was a contest for articles dealing with environmental, political, and social issues. The contest had not crossed her mind, but Pete's confidence brought a huge grin to her face.

Nov. 1, 2009
Thursday. Best day of the week. Submitting the Orphans'
Awareness article today to Colorado Writes. Can't wait to tell Will
today! He will be thrilled.

Several Thursdays passed. Kayla was bursting with her news, but every week it seemed that Will was having a hard day. One week he was sick, the other he was worried over issues with Celia. Another week he was frustrated with homework. Kayla decided to wait until December to tell him. By that time the finalists would be announced, and if she didn't qualify, it was better that he didn't know.

It was the Wednesday before Thanksgiving when Kayla realized she hadn't made a plan for Will with the holiday. Kayla's family had invited her to spend the day with them, and she totally forgot that the holiday would coincide with her weekly meeting with Will. She drove over to the Green House after work. It was 5:05 p.m. when she pulled up to the house. As her car slowed to a stop, a fifteen passenger van with all the children packed inside drove off. She recognized Will, Catch, and Celia in the back seat. After getting out of the car, she stood in the street a bit confused. *Where are they going? It's nearly dark out. Something just doesn't seem right.* Curious thoughts swarmed as she turned to look at the empty house. Taking a few steps into the yard, she remembered the wall plaque that read: "Green House." The whole neighborhood was silent. The sun would be completely gone within twenty minutes. The dusk light made it seem as if the whole house was sitting in a shadow. A chilly breeze whistled in her ears.

It occurred to her that she never remembered seeing any official documentation on the wall stating that the house was an orphanage. Maybe they were all foster kids. Maybe she just didn't see it. With all the research from her paper at the forefront of her mind, she walked up to the front porch. The wooden steps creaked under her feet. The spring on the rusting screen door screeched as she opened and held it with her foot. In front of her was an old metal door handle. She slowly extended her hand forward. Locked. She stepped aside to the window, forgetting the screen door, which made a startlingly loud slam shut. She jumped as the whacking sound of the door echoed down the street. She looked in the window, which was covered on the inside by a bed sheet with a 70's floral pattern. There was a little slit on the side where the sheet had been pulled aside, and she could peek in the window. The house was dark, but she could see the disarray of old toys, and a few of her stuffed animals that she had given the children nearly a year before. Her eyes strained to see Will's Broncos jacket draped on the couch. *Why wouldn't he have brought that? He wears it everywhere he goes. And it's freezing out here,* she wondered. With a step back, she looked up around the frame of the house, but the change in perspective made her aware of a figure that stood in her line of sight. It was a middle-aged man in dirty jeans with holes in the knees. He had silver hair that had been cut short, and he wore a dingy red flannel shirt. She didn't know what to say or do. She walked to her car, as the man made slow steps toward her. Her heart raced and she peeled the car out as she drove off. The man stood in the yard, shaking his head at her.

The next day Kayla did not come to see Will. She went

to her parents' house in the mid morning. The home was filled with life. The refrigerator was covered with Thanksgiving art crafts made by the Rachel's children, as well as pictures from their Thanksgiving production. Kayla smiled to see her nieces and nephew dressed as pilgrims and Indians. The children played games while adults munched on a table full of hors d'oeurves. Though it was fun to hear all the family news and stories, Kayla couldn't get her mind off of Will. It bothered her that he had left his jacket. She wondered what kind of Thanksgiving dinner he would be eating that day. A couple times her dad or Ricky sat down next to her and quietly asked if she was OK. This year she felt like she had more to be thankful for than she ever had, but she still felt a painful brokenness in her heart. The void within her before was just a self-driven sorrow. On this Thanksgiving, her heart was actually hurting for someone else, and it hurt all the more because she didn't know how to help Will or any of the little ones living at the Green House.

---

Dec. 1, 2009

I got it! In all the articles submitted to Colorado Writes, mine was chosen in the top five to be featured at their annual banquet. I don't believe it! They announced it on their website, and sent out an email. YES!!!! I just can't believe it. Wish I could tell Will. Oh, Will. I wonder how he is. I wish he was here to celebrate.

# CHAPTER □ 13

>>>>>>>>>>>>>>>>

IT was a rare occasion that Kayla ever missed the evening news. She would have told anyone in the office that it was a sorry excuse for journalism with all the obvious bias and personal opinion. Any proud journalist in the newsroom naturally looked down his nose at the media of television news reports. But behind closed doors, in the privacy of her one bedroom apartment, Kayla enjoyed cooking dinner and watching the evening news. It reminded her of childhood days when her mom prepared dinner for the family. Her dad watched the 6:00 news every night in the next room. Kayla felt at home with the sounds of sizzling garlic in a skillet coupled with the chiming of news reports in the background. It put her at ease. Kayla hummed to herself as she stirred sliced squash and zucchini over the stove. Jack lay content on the floor in the middle of the kitchen and Kayla rubbed his belly with one of her bare feet.

Over the weekend, her article was narrowed to the final five in the contest, and she had been invited to the banquet. On that Monday morning, Pete made an announcement to the

whole office and his voice beamed with pride as he congratulated Kayla in front of her colleagues. It had been a great day,
but that evening all was brought to a halt. The news ran as usual
with the typical array of reports, but a frightful headline caught
Kayla's attention.

"Girl with mysterious background found dead. Yesterday, two baggage handlers found an unidentified teenage girl
dead in the dumpster at Denver International Airport." Kayla
turned to see the television screen, and dropped her spatula
on Jack's head when she saw the pale and lifeless shot of a very
familiar face.

"Celia." Kayla moved toward the television and covered
her mouth as the story continued.

"Authorities are still conducting investigations regarding time of death and suspects involved. However, the case took
a confusing twist when DNA samples linked the girl to a family living in Colorado Springs. Apparently the victim's genetic
makeup was a perfect match to a brother whose samples were
in the police database for unspecified reasons from his youth.
When Channel Nine reporters approached the family about
the DNA match, they appeared confused and denied ever having a daughter." The front door of a suburban home appeared
on screen with a reporter asking questions of a couple in their
late thirties.

"Mr. and Mrs. Frederick Lowman gave a frustrated yet
firm answer that they never had a daughter," the news anchor
continued. Kayla stared in awe as she watched the statements
from the Lowmans.

"We only have one son. We have never had a daughter.
Never. This is obviously a mistake."

"Can you tell us how exactly, then, there can be a perfect DNA match between your son and this dead girl found in

Denver? DNA doesn't lie, Mr. Lowman. This girl, whether you like it or not, is somehow connected to your family. She's dead, sir, and figuring out your connection to this girl may help find her killers." Finally the wife spoke up.

"Will you people just leave us alone? Don't you think I know how many kids I have? I've never had a girl. I've never had a…"

Right there on television, Mrs. Lowman's eyes widened. Her mouth dropped slightly as though she saw a ghost. She couldn't seem to finish her sentence. The husband put an arm around his wife and asked the reporter to leave.

"Where is she?"

"Huh? Who?" Will was out of breath and confused. Kayla had showed up at his front door completely unannounced.

"You know who. Celia!" Kayla asked with growing ferocity. Will frantically looked side to side and sensed a menacing glance from the Father who was watching television on the couch. He immediately hurried down the steps and walked down the street while Kayla followed behind him. He whispered out the side of his mouth and took quick steps approaching the stop sign on the corner.

"What kinda stupid are you? I could get torn up because of your loose mouth!" The two turned down another street, but Will did not slow down. They walked silently with speed in their steps. Kayla kept losing her footing as she turned while trying to get a good gaze at Will who walked with missional fire. His eyes remained on the uneven sidewalk before him.

"What is going on?"

"Why do you think I know anything?"

"What happened to Celia?"

"I wish I could tell you, but I don't know anything."

"Come on, Will. You gotta know something. You loved her."

"Nah. I don't think I…"

"Will, she was like the only real family you had. What kind of brother doesn't care when his sister ends up in a dumpster?"

"The one who doesn't want to sleep in a dumpster either."

"You seriously expect me to believe that you don't know anything?" Will's eyes started to water. He clenched his teeth and his face turned red. Kayla softened at the sight of this lonely kid grieving over his sister. Since the night before, when she saw Celia's dead body on the evening news, she had completely forgotten about Will's brokenness. She reached her hand out to his shoulder, but he pulled back. "Look, I'm sorry, Will. I didn't mean to be such a jerk. I just… I want to… I just think there's more to all this than meets the eye."

"What more do you want to know? They traded her off. When she put up a fight, they got freaked out over the scene she was making. She was already pretty beat up, and they said she was more trouble than she was worth." Will wiped tears from his cheeks.

"Who's 'they'?" Will gave no response. "There's still more, Will."

"I told you everything. I'll probably get axed for this." Will turned and started walking down the street.

"There's more, Will." He kept walking. "They found her parents." Will stopped. "Don't you watch the news? Well, whatever, you probably missed it. They matched her DNA to her real family." Will turned.

"That's not possible."

"The family denied that she even existed. What's that about?"

"Done. This is done, Kayla. Don't get into it." Will walked off and didn't stop. Maybe he knew, but she sensed fear and danger in the air. He would not be her source, but she knew she had to find the answers, for his sake.

The Lowmans were not thrilled to see another reporter. Kayla had dressed up, stood as tall as she could and wore her Denver Post badge. Mr. Lowman peeked through a sliver of an open door.

"Please go away. My family has had enough."

"Mr. Lowman, please. I am from The Denver Post, and I..."

"No more reporters, lady. We're done with all this."

"Mr. Lowman, you must know something..."

"No, no, NO! How many times do I have to tell you people? We only have one kid. One son. That's it. I don't know that girl."

"But, Mr. Lowman, I do. I know her. I *knew* her. And I saw a look in your wife's eyes on TV that made me think maybe she knew her, too." The man's stance softened, and a gentle hand reached over his shoulder. Mr. Lowman stepped aside as his wife moved forward.

"What did you say your name was?" the woman asked. Kayla extended a handshake with a compassionate smile.

"Kayla Barrington, ma'am."

The Lowmans welcomed Kayla in, but didn't offer anything more than their couch and some apprehensive conversation. Kayla carefully guarded the details of how she knew Celia, but she also tried to reveal the lovely side of this young girl. She wanted to prove to the Lowmans that she did know their daughter. They needed to understand that Celia was real, whether they chose to believe so, or not.

"So, you didn't ever have a baby and put her up for adoption? No children that died or were abducted? No chance a baby could have gotten mixed up in the hospital? No repressed memories? I am sorry, Mrs. Lowman, I am just trying to think of any and every possibility for why this girl could be related to you."

"I am sorry, but we only have one son. Always have," Mrs. Lowman said. Kayla sat quietly with her journal in her lap.

"Did you ever live in Denver?"

"Well, yes, just outside of Denver. That's where I grew up. We moved to the Springs about fifteen years ago, then our son was born."

"Where was that, exactly?" Kayla asked. She sat with her hands on her lap. It seemed like a dead-end.

"Babson." Mrs. Lowman said. Kayla's eyes widened.

"Where did you say?"

"Babson."

"I know this is really personal. And I thank you so much for your time. But, you just had the one pregnancy?"

"Well, actually... I was pregnant one other time, but it was an accident. It was stupid..."

"That's enough." Mr. Lowman put a hand on her knee as though to stifle her words.

"It's not enough." Mrs. Lowman looked at Kayla. "Do you have kids?"

"No, ma'am."

"Well, a mother always knows. She just knows. The

baby was from one stupid night when John and I had too much to drink. We got engaged once we found out, and we were gonna keep the baby, but the reality was, we just weren't ready to be parents." Mrs. Lowman sniffled and wiped away tears that seemed to be long overdue.

"So, you…"

"We chose." Mr. Lowman stood abruptly. "Twenty years ago, we chose. And I think, it's time that you quit meddling in our personal lives, and went on your way." Mr. Lowman stood up and gave a guiding hand directing Kayla to the door.

"Celia is dead."

Josh's eyes grew concerned. Kayla had immediately driven to the church after leaving the Lowman's home. She made it just in time for the closing prayer of the Wednesday night service and managed to pull Josh aside before he was caught up with other people. Josh set up a blanket on the couch in his office for his daughter. A video and some cookies kept her occupied, and Josh offered a handful of cookies to Kayla as she walked into the office lobby. Before Josh could even sit down, Kayla blurted out her news as though she had been choking on it all night. He was stunned.

"Oh, Kayla, I am so sorry."

"Me, too."

"How'd you find out? What happened?"

"The T.V. news. Some people found her in a dumpster at DIA." Josh swallowed slowly and slowly sunk into the wing-back chair behind him. He put the other cookies on the arm of the chair.

"Wow. How's Will?"

"Not great." She sat silently for a moment. "Thing is, there's more to this."

"What do you mean?"

"They found her parents. DNA's cool that way, ya' know?"

"Really? Wow, well, that's good, right?"

"No, they denied she ever existed." Josh sat still with squinted eyes and a furrowed brow.

"Well, how…"

"I don't know. I talked to them and…"

"You talked to them?"

"Yeah, they live in the Springs. So, I went over this afternoon. And I asked every question I could think of. There's gotta be a connection. There's something in this that is pulling it all together. I just can't figure it out. I have racked my brain over and over. And there's only one thing I can figure. And it doesn't even make sense. I don't know how, but it's all I've got."

"What is it?"

"She grew up in Babson." She could hardly breathe out of fear for where the conversation would end up. "And she had an abortion." Both Josh and Kayla were quiet. They could hear the muffled sounds of cartoons in the next room.

"And?"

"And this is the only clinic there ever was in this town. This property," she said.

"I see."

"Look, I know it's a sin and all the church people call it murder and it's so horrible. But really, this place is the only connection I have between Celia and her parents. What is that about?" Kayla feared she might have offended Josh. He wasn't looking at her. He didn't seem to be looking at anything. He just sat there. Then a lump tightened in her throat at a painful thought that had never occurred to her. "Don't tell me you didn't know this place was an abortion clinic? Don't they have to tell you that stuff when you are buying a place?" She swallowed hard and felt sick to her stomach. Now she really wished she had never come to this wretched place. Ever. Fourteen years ago, months ago, tonight. Nothing good had come from all this. "Josh?" His eyes blinked and then looked up into hers.

"Kayla, I know exactly what this place was." His eyes were red and his cheeks looked splotchy as he held tears back. She had never seen him so undone before, and she felt horrible for assuming he was blind to the history of this building. "I know what happened here. We all do. I grew up in this town. We all knew what this place was. I remember the day the clinic closed. I drove past the vacant building every day for years on my way to work. It wasn't but a few years ago that our church had out grown its facility, and we were searching for a new place to worship. I don't know how to explain it, but my heart was drawn to this place. It was drawn to all the brokenness it represented. And I couldn't think of any better place to worship God. What better place for God to restore all that was lost? Yeah, some of the church folks were upset about it, but nearly everyone was on board. It's been a passionate cry of this church to help people in need, and that's not to exclude anyone." Kayla looked away. She feared he could supernaturally read her mind, or see her past. Insecurity wrapped around her, but she pushed through to focus on Celia.

"Look, I don't know what good it is to come back to this place, but I keep thinking… I don't know, I've gotta' figure this thing out with Celia. And this is the only place I know to go."

"Well then… for Celia," he said. Josh stood in front of her and stuck his hands in his pockets. His voice hushed as though letting her in on a secret. "Come with me." Josh walked quickly down the hallway, through the lobby and up to the front of the sanctuary. Dee Ann was collecting stray papers in the seats and Josh gave a quiet word in her direction. "Hey Dee, we will be downstairs for a few minutes." Dee Ann looked up with surprise. Her eyes followed them as she crumpled extra leaflets and papers in her fist. To the left of the stage was a door painted the same color as the wall.

"Where are we going?"

"Mattie's favorite hiding spot," he said without looking back at her.

The door led to a prayer room with a few stackable cushioned chairs. A Bible sat on an end table and a small lamp lit the room warmly. The walls were covered with a khaki colored velvet fabric hanging on decorative rods fastened at the ceiling.

"I would think that Mattie could do better than this," Kayla said. Josh smiled and conceded.

"You must know her well. Yeah, this is a prayer room that's always available whenever the church is open." Josh walked to the opposite side of the room and reached behind the fabric. "Most people think the curtains are for sound proofing. And they do serve that purpose." Josh revealed a hidden door behind the thick fabric. Opening the door, Josh proceeded down a flight of wooden steps. He pulled a string above his head that flicked on a hanging light bulb, which lit the path before him. The stairs creaked with each step and the air was cooler down in the lower level. At the bottom of the steps to her left, was a makeshift tent or fort creation made with old linens and outdated medical equipment. Kayla stepped carefully toward the tent. A bulky medical lampstand was aimed to shine light in Mattie's fort. Plugging it into the wall, the blinding light was familiar and reminded Kayla of her experience at the clinic many years before.

"Is this where you do a lot of your counseling? In your tent?" Kayla said. Josh smiled without a witty response to throw back. Turning to the right, Kayla was greeted by a ransacked heap of office files and papers. The basement was easily 25 feet by 40 feet. And half of the room was covered in sloppy piles of paperwork that measured taller than her knees. "What's all this?"

"History," Josh said. Kayla walked toward the paper. Handwritten names were written in bold marker on the outside of each file folder. Josh sat on the stairs. "When the clinic closed down, I heard it happened because of shady stuff, and the owners were run out of town. I guess they left in such a rush, that they didn't mind leaving all this behind. I don't know what you are hoping to find. Maybe Celia was cloned or DNA was taken for stem cell research. I don't know, but anything you want to know about anyone who ever walked in the door…" He gestured to the massive pile. "It's here."

Kayla was stunned. No words could express it. She was conflicted with anger that she had never found this place before. Yet, she also felt ecstatic that somewhere buried in that pile she might find clues to not only solve the mysteries of Celia's death, but she might even find some true closure in her life as well. She knelt down on the floor beside the edge of the pile and slowly traced her fingers along the edge of one of the file folders.

"It was nearly a year before we found this stuff. Mattie was in this phase where she would hide in all sorts of odd places. Kind of like she was playing hide-n-seek without letting us know about it. One day I sent Dee Ann off to find her. She came back with eyes about as big as yours right now. It felt like a buried treasure in a morbid sort of way. Dee Ann helped Mattie set up her fort, and together we spent the whole afternoon digging through files, weeping, and praying." Josh looked over at Kayla who was now entranced by the mountain of papers. "Well, maybe your answers are in here somewhere. Where do we get started?"

All Kayla could think about was finding her file. She wished a tornado would pick all the papers up and leave hers behind. Josh started to move toward the papers, but Kayla's cloud of insecurity loomed over her head. At this point, he didn't even know that her story was part of his hidden treasure, and she wanted to keep it that way.

"Actually, I uhh, I hate for you to leave Mattie up there. Why don't you check on her? I can get to searching here." Josh appreciated the sentiment, but continued toward the heavy stacks.

"Hey, don't worry about it. VeggieTales has her occupied, and we can make better headway together."

"Please," Kayla pleaded with a desperate quiver in her voice. She whispered the tender request. "Please, this is something I need to do. Please, let me do this alone." Josh looked into her eyes. He was a gentleman, and he would wait patiently.

"No problem," he said with a nod of his head. Josh stood up and brushed his hands on his pants. No words were needed. He just turned and went back up the steps.

Kayla felt as though she sat in the middle of an ancient tomb. She stared at what was like an ocean of pain. It reminded her of when she visited the Holocaust museum and saw piles of shoes, or a mountain of hair. Somehow the depth and height created by the collaboration of such small little things sent a rushing wave of sobriety over her. Moment's later Kayla's mission became very clear. Find it. She must find it. Her fingers moved fast, shuffling over and over again. File after file. No rhyme or order. It was not alphabetical; it was not by date of the procedure. Sometimes as she moved to another stack the last pile toppled over which spilled ultrasound pictures, receipts, and papers.

Kayla moved faster with increased fervor. Eventually, she was completely surrounded by files. She inched closer on her knees and rearranged the stacks of paper. No sign of Mrs. Lowman's or her own file. Hours passed. Her back ached. Her fingers felt dirty after handling so many dusty pages. She kept glancing at her watch. Midnight approached. The pile was thinning out. Desperation syncopated her breathing pattern. Searching. Searching. She started to second-guess herself. *Was I moving too quickly? Was I not thorough enough? Did I pass it over?*

With only a few piles left, Kayla's pace slowed down. Her brow furrowed with tension. Hope was depleted. As each minute passed, more despair crept over her. *With my luck, it will be the last one in the pile,* she thought. Jumping over the pile in front of her, she crawled to the edge of the ominous paper sea. Her hands stretched to the bottom of the pile to reach the very last file she might have picked up. Her heart raced. As she pulled the file out from the bottom, the others atop it slid to the floor and fanned out beside her. She pulled the file up and read the name on the tab. FISCHER, JAN.

Warm tears blurred her vision. Inhaling the cold air felt painful. She ran her hands through her hair and arched her back to get a good stretch. Looking up at the ceiling, she let out a frustrated cry. She wiped the tears from her cheeks with dusty hands, and returned to the last few stacks of files. Still searching. Still hoping, yet so fearful. *What does this mean? That it didn't happen? Am I crazy? Did I just dream up the last fifteen years of misery? WHY? Why isn't it here?!* Her mind raced with questions. Papers surrounded her. Once again, she had hit a dead end. She pulled her knees up to her chest and sobbed. Tears drenched her pants.

The sound of footsteps creaking on the stairs startled her. She sniffed back her congested nose. It was only a minute later that Josh was stood before her.

"What's wrong? You couldn't find her file? Maybe if I help, what was the name of the lady again?" Josh knelt down at the edge of the pile and started pulling files onto his lap. Kayla just shook her head without stopping. He looked up at her. "What?" he asked. With childlike tears, she didn't worry about his opinion of her. She just burst with sorrow.

"Do you really think I come here to get close to God, or something? Do you really think I am on some spiritual journey, some quest? Or that I was ever doing research for an article?" Her face was flushed and soaked with tears. "This is why I come here." She spread her arms out over the hedge of files. "Because, this is me. I am this. I am *in* this. Somewhere, my story is in this pile." She waited, but Josh did not offer a response. "Or atleast, I should be in here. I can't find my file. I've searched for hours, and everything I've hated about myself is missing."

Josh sat quietly, sadly. She felt an ugly separation between them, which ironically was due to the pile of her past before her. A minute passed. Then something new sparked in Josh's eyes.

"How far along were you? When you had it done?" Josh asked. Kayla grew defensive, and didn't see a point in his nosy questions.

"Why?"

"Just… when?"

"I was just about thirty weeks," she said. Josh's face dropped.

"Oh. Then maybe I can help. There were some... well, you just have to see."

He walked over to the far side of the basement where Mattie's tent was set up. One side of the tent had a bed sheet draped over a gray filing cabinet and a medical lamp. This floor lamp was more than five feet tall and had a large base. Its bulb was the shape of a 12-inch saucer and was the type used in a delivery room to shine on the patient. Josh opened the file cabinet and the screeching sound of metal against metal sent chills up Kayla's spine. The drawer leaned to one side and bowed outward with files packed tightly, brimming at the top. Names in the same color marker and same handwriting filled the tabs.

"What's this?"

"Dee Ann and I noticed something one day. There were a lot of babies who were in the third trimester when the procedure was done. Some women were at 27 weeks; others were up to 35 weeks. We collected these files as we found them. One at a time, this cabinet was filled." He reached down and pulled open the bottom drawer, also crammed full. "I don't know what this is for, or why, but I think this is part of why the clinic was shut down. If you were as far along as you said, then your name is probably in here, too."

Adrenaline flooded through Kayla's core as she walked toward the small cabinet. Josh disassembled Mattie's tent, draping a few of the sheets and blankets on the neck of the medical lamp. Bent down on her knees, Kayla's hands hovered over the musty manila tabs. The basement steps creaked, and Kayla peeked over her shoulder as Dee Ann approached. No one said anything. No one needed to. Josh gripped an armload of files and passed them to Kayla.

She sat on the floor flipping through files, looking for her name. Dee Ann rubbed Kayla's back for a moment while she, too, squatted down to sit on the floor. Josh plopped another stack at their side, as they continued the search. Moments later, the cabinet slammed shut, and the women flinched while looking up to see that he only had one file in his hand. It was surreal to see her name in bold capital letters.

BARRINGTON, KAYLA.

It felt as though that name represented another person. For years she felt inescapably tied to this file, this moment, this procedure, and now she felt distant, like a stranger looking in.

Opening it up, she saw the initial forms filled out on the day of the procedure. She flipped through the pages and saw her signature in various places. Her handwriting looked younger, it was shaky, scared. Behind these pages was another medical form with an ultrasound picture that was attached to the top with a paperclip. She stared at the black and white photo. It was the baby's profile. Large tears rolled over her cheekbones, and she caught them in her hand before they hit the pages in her lap. She wiped her hands on her pants and gently caressed the cheek of her baby on the picture.

*I'm sorry, Blanche. I'm so sorry.* Moving the picture aside, she focused on the paperwork before her. It all seemed to be pretty standard stuff with a lot of medical terms, the time of the procedure, a list of anesthetics that were used, with various acronyms. This was the last page, but it felt incomplete. As she closed the file, she noticed colored ink on the back of the last page she had just looked at. Opening the file back up, she found handwritten notes on the back of the medical form. In the top corner it read:

19in., 5lbs. 06oz.
Normal. (XY)
>>> GREEN HOUSE/ DEN.

Josh leaned over to read the markings upside down. "What is that?" he asked.

In the bottom right corner were more scribbles:

$10,000 per CODE 01014, Schleck.

**T. WILLIAMS- Streetcar > Blanche

ID Track: 592B, c/o WILL per Angel.

"What's that stuff?" Josh asked while pointing to the bottom corner.

"I told the nurse that I was naming the girl, Blanche, after that play *A Streetcar Named Desire.*" Kayla studied the handwriting a bit more, and noticed the signature reading "Angel" was the last thing in the bottom corner. Maybe Angel was the person who wrote it all down. She stretched her memory as hard as she could. Flashes of the images of each nurse came flooding to her mind. She remembered the nurses in the waiting rooms, in the prep rooms, at the front desk. And then she remembered the image of a gold angel shaped pin attached to someone's scrubs. She closed her eyes straining for more.

She remembered being in the room for surgery. She was on the bed, nurses were checking her vitals. They all had masks covering their faces. All of them but one. It was her. She remembered as things were getting dark and scary, that beautiful angelic nurse rubbed her face and her hair. That woman whispered in a low voice that all would be OK and over soon. That woman wore an angel pin. That must have been her.

Kayla looked at Angel's handwriting. *What was she saying? What was she doing?* Kayla noticed the line above. Angel had circled the letters W-I-L-L on the word Williams. Then below, she had written and underlined the word WILL again after an ID number. Her thoughts veered to the familiar dream, which had haunted her for years.

*A bright light shone over her and the sounds of voices echoed eerily. Her body felt heavy and laid flat in the bed as though she had been paralyzed. People were working busily around her, but she couldn't quite see what was going on.*

*"Here we go. Almost there." The doctor's voice coaxed the team. Then, soon after, the cry of a newborn baby soared through the room. "Here he is! He's arrived!" Kayla's vision was fuzzy but a warm light glowed as the man lifted a tiny naked baby in the air.*

Seamlessly the vision of the dashboard dream rolled before her eyes. The scene where she nearly hit Will with her car on the street started to fit into place. *How could I have dreamed of someone I had never met?* She had often asked herself who this boy was, and why he visited her dreams night after night. All she could hear was the resonating screech of her car breaks skidding on the road. The sound of Will's hands slamming the hood of the car felt like a violent jolt in her spirit that brought immediate clarity to her mind.

"Woah! Oh, oh," Kayla spoke in a low, sickly tone in the midst of her nervous epiphany. She shot up, flung the papers, and paced around in the basement.

"What? Tell us!" Josh pleaded as he organized the papers strewn on the floor.

"It wasn't a dream. I know it wasn't. It was real. It happened." She put her hand to her stomach that now felt queasy.

"What happened?" Dee Ann asked.

"It's him. I know it is. I know it like I know my name. It's him. He's him."

"Kayla, you aren't making any sense." Kayla rushed over

to the papers and picked up the ultrasound picture as well as the paper with Angel's writing on it.

"I don't know what they did, or how they did it, but that baby was not aborted. I've dreamed about my baby being born for fifteen years. I always thought it was a dream. It was real, a memory," she turned to look them each in the eyes, "it was real." She held the picture and the paper right in front of Josh's face, shaking them emphatically. Josh sat back against the wall taking it all in. Dee Ann covered her mouth in shock. They wanted to believe her, but it still didn't make sense.

"I'm telling you, Josh. Look at this paper. Why would they put a length and weight? What's this ID number? And this dollar amount? What is that about?" Josh took hold of the paper and studied it closely.

"I thought you said you had a girl."

"That's what they told me. The only ultrasound I ever had was here at this clinic. The only people who ever told me the baby's gender was the nurse in this building. I just believed it. What if it wasn't a girl?"

"Look, this notation here, it says "XY", maybe I'm reading too much into this, but maybe that's code for the baby being a boy." Dee Ann pointed at the writing on the page.

"Let's look at the other files and compare them. Maybe we will learn something about these notes." Kayla grabbed more files from the floor.

"Good idea."

For the next hour, the three researched more than half of the files, stacking them, by gender, on top of the filing cabinet. Each page had a birth weight and height, and all were identified with either an "XX" or "XY." Dee Ann's connection on this code was affirmed by the names noted in the bottom left corner just next to Angel's signature. Female names always had an "XX" on their file, and the boys had an "XY." Underneath the "XY" code, a hand drawn arrow pointed to five different titles. Kayla's had read: "Green House/ DEN." Josh kept a list of the other titles that included: Blue Balls, Yellow Banana, Red Head, and Rainbow Fever. The Blue Balls and Rainbow Fever were both followed with DEN. Red Head was followed by the letters STL, and Yellow Banana had LASV NV. All the color oriented notations also matched the color highlighter used on the outside of the file tab. Josh started to talk out his thoughts.

"These are places. They have to be. Look, DEN stands for Denver. STL is St. Louis. And this one is for Las Vegas, Nevada."

Some of the files had a large red marker strike-through on the notes. A red scribble next to the "X" said T.O.D. and a date.

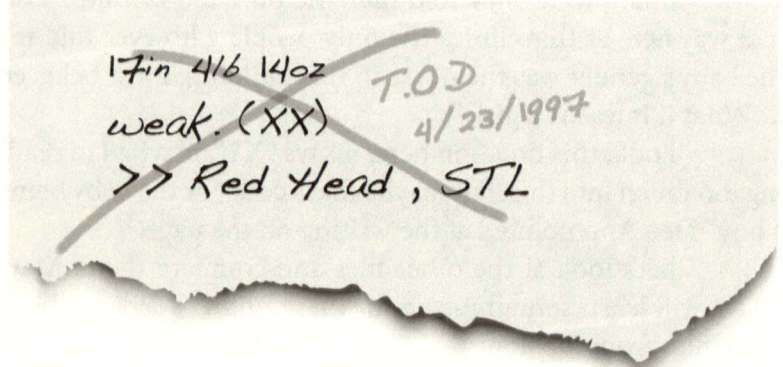

"This one didn't make it." Kayla pointed to the red markings. "The date for the procedure was a week before this date in red." She looked down at the other files in her lap. The one marked in red did not have a dollar amount on it. She picked up the other files in her lap.

"These numbers here. Girls are always higher. Boys are

a little lower. What if this whole page is actually a…"

"Receipt." Josh interrupted her, and they both knew the other's assumptions. They looked at one another with heavy hearts. No one wanted to admit it. Not even speak it. Kayla dropped the files to the floor paced the room.

"How could this happen?" Josh picked up more files and flipped through them. "How could the clinic get away with this? I mean the implications here are huge. How is it that no one caught on to this?" Josh studied the papers.

Kayla stood next to the cabinet, staring at the empty drawer, and the lopsided stack of evidence.

"Shame… I guess," she said. Josh and Dee Ann looked at her. They knew she was not answering out of speculation, but from experience. "Abortions aren't exactly first-date conversation material with your college crush. You don't talk about it. You don't tell people. You already feel judged. By people, Christians… God. And you don't want any more of it. You'd never tell another woman. Every time I spoke with a woman who had kids, I feared she could see right through me. Like she knew everything, like she could see me with my own eyes." Kayla didn't look up. She couldn't. Her stomach was in knots and she felt the weight of her decision all over again.

"Kayla." Josh leaned in and waited for her to look at him. "I am so sorry for all that you have endured. Sorry for it all; but don't think you have to hold all this in your hands. It's not yours to carry by yourself." He paused and looked at the files before them. "There is hope for the future. God's heart never projects shame. People do that, not God. There is hope… even for this."

With a slow nod of her head, Kayla swiftly thrust the top cabinet drawer shut. It echoed in the room, and sent the stack of files awkwardly plummeting onto the medical lamp.

She stumbled to catch the files, but tripped and fell with all her body weight in the same direction. She hit the heavy medical lamp. A domino effect sent the files, Kayla, and the lamp plunging into the wall.

"Oh! I am so sorry!" Kayla rubbed the tender spot where her head hit the lamp. Josh and Dee Ann jumped up to help Kayla, but Josh's eyes were locked on something behind her. The head of the lamp broke through a piece of the wall.

"That's odd," he said. Kayla pulled the lamp out of the wall, and Josh touched the edge of the wall. It was made of a thin plaster. He stuck his nose into the hole, his eyes widened, and he coughed on the dust in the air. Pulling at the wall, pieces of plaster crumbled to the floor.

"What is it?" Kayla looked over his shoulder.

"A room. I can't see..." Josh responded while peering further. Dee Ann repositioned the medical lamp to shine into the jagged opening.

Kayla gasped as light dimly exposed a dusty room filled with more equipment. Lined side by side were eight tiny incubator bassinets. The kind one might see in a maternity ward at a hospital. A counter top on the far end of the room held an infant scale. A stainless steel tray beside the scale was piled with surgical tools. In the corner, tall metal poles had empty I.V. bags attached. Two bulky machines had coiled paper discharged on the floor with heart monitor readings printed across it. The Plexiglas frames on the bassinets were unmistakable; a few had tiny oxygen masks draped over the side. Receiving blankets were strewn on the padding in the incubators. One preemie sized knitted cap lay on the floor.

# CHAPTER □ 14

>>>>>>>>>>>>>>

"WHAT are you going to do?" Josh called Kayla the next day as she drove across town to the usual Subway to meet Will.

"Don't you think I have asked myself that question a thousand times since I woke up this morning?"

"I'm not trying to pester you, but you are on your way to see him right now, right? So, it's like D-Day in minus twenty minutes. You can't just walk up and say, "Hey, dude, I'm your mom.""

Kayla gripped the steering wheel with one hand and stretched out the arm with her cell phone as though throwing it out the window. He was right, but she didn't know what to do.

"Well, all morning I looked up information about kids being sold for money. They call it human trafficking, but it is mostly reported in foreign countries. Like impoverished places with lots of brothels and slums."

"You think that's what happened to Will?"

"What else could it be? All those files? Each with a receipt noted on the back. And the medical equipment for infants? That was like a whole NICU floor hidden down there. Why would a clinic like that need equipment to sustain life? And why would they plaster fake walls to hide it? It would not have been that hard for them to nurture infants born in the third trimester into stability. Preemies are born all the time. And what a perfect set up! As far as the whole world was concerned, these babies didn't even exist. So they were sold as... slaves. Like property." Just hearing her own words spoken aloud made her want to scream in fury. Josh let out a disgusted sigh.

"This can't be happening. It can't."

"That's what I have been saying all morning," Kayla said. "I just keep thinking, this is America, for cryin' out loud! Land of the free. As sad as it is, I can see this stuff happening in third world countries, but the fact that it's happening here, in my town... it just makes me sick. I am a part of it, and I didn't even know. It makes me want to lash out or hit something. It can't be happening, but it is happening. It *is*, Josh. And the more I learn about it, the more I realize that that this is a bigger issue our country needs to fight against. And I am standing right in the middle of it." She gripped the steering wheel tighter with angry desperation.

"So, are you going to tell him you are his mom?"

"I don't know. I think that's too much to take in. Maybe I can just be an ally for him, tell him about this trafficking stuff. Just get him out first."

"Yeah, that's good. Just do what you gotta do." Kayla pulled into the parking lot and saw Will sitting on the curb outside Subway. He wore his Broncos jacket.

For months she had watched this boy grow. He was taller, stronger, becoming a man. He excelled in his schoolwork and grew more trusting of Kayla. Such trust was vital on this day, but it wasn't strong enough when weighed against Kayla's news.

"Are you crazy? You're trying to tell me I'm a slave? Do I look like a slave to you?"

"Will, just listen…"

"No, you listen! You don't even know what you are talking about. I can do whatever I want."

"Really? Will, look at me. I am not trying to make you feel bad. I just want to help."

"Help? You think coming to my house without warning is help? You think that showing up at dusk and snooping around the house is help?"

"How'd you know about that? I was coming to see you, and you all drove off in a van. What was that about? Where were you going?"

"You really wanna know? Really?! Where Catch got his name? How Celia died? It's just a business, Kayla. Sex. Me and all the kids, and whoever shows up. Every night. Catch-All always ends up with the STDs and it's a wonder he can even work and keep the guys happy. Celia was like a sister to me, and they sold her off like a piece of furniture on Craig's List. I can't change it. I couldn't help her. It's just the way it is."

Will was fiery, and raw, and she had never seen his eyes so fierce. Kayla softened and she spoke slowly in a whisper.

"But it doesn't have to be that way, Will. It's not right. You don't deserve this." Will shook his head and tears formed around his eyes. "Please, Will, your life doesn't have to be like this. We can get you out." Will's lip quivered and he looked down at his half-eaten sandwich. The reality of all that was weighing on his shoulders was suddenly too hard to bear.

"You don't know these guys, Kayla. You don't know who they know. You don't know what they're capable of. They won't just come after me, but you, too. And I can't..." Will's voice cracked, and he covered his mouth. He cleared his throat a few times. Without a chance for Kayla to stop him, he jumped out of his seat, ran out the door and across the parking lot.

"Will, please!" Kayla fumbled as Will disappeared around a corner. She returned to her seat with the lunches still sitting on the table. Will was protecting her. He couldn't protect Celia, but he was trying to protect Kayla. She stared at his fountain soda and leftovers. It was not his job to protect her. It never had been. And if there was anything in those wrappers that could prove that, then maybe she could usurp her role that had been abandoned fifteen years earlier.

Dec. 7, 2009

Totally sick to my stomach. Yesterday I told Will, but he didn't believe me. It's like he's brainwashed. Like he was reciting something that had been beaten into him. Like it wasn't even him talking. So, yesterday I called the Cops. Reported the house. Police got there after dark. The house was abandoned, but not like packed up, just like they all left. Cops hung around all night but no one ever came home. Maybe someone tipped them off. I don't know. Police are still keeping watch on the house, nothing is turning up. Have I lost him? Did I do the wrong thing? Why didn't I see this earlier? How can this be happening? This is Denver, not Thailand. This just shouldn't be happening!!!! GRRR!!!!

⟶ I also took Will's stuff to the police. Evan has a friend from college who works in the lab. Evan said they could get DNA results ASAP. They said it's usually two weeks, but sometimes sooner. Gave them my cell. Waiting. Just waiting.

Tossing. Turning. All Kayla could hear were the magnified sounds of her bed sheets crumpling with her every move. She rolled over again and again. Jack was clearly frustrated with her sporadic restlessness as he jumped off the bed and flopped down in her closet. She counted sheep, sang songs in her head, and sang out loud. Her eyelids burned even when closed, and she couldn't keep them shut for more than a few minutes at a time.

Awareness; that is all it was. Before, she had only heard of orphans, the homeless, the underprivileged, and now, children forced into sexual acts with brutal strangers. She knew that people in desperate situations existed. They were there before, but remained faceless. She didn't know their names or their stories. And even as she lay on her soft bed, she still didn't know them. But she knew one. Will. And she remembered the faces of the young ones in his house. She remembered the smile of that sweet little girl, May. While she struggled for a comfortable position on her queen bed, cloaked by a feather duvet, Will fought for survival in the darkest pit of human suffering. She stared at the ceiling and stewed over the nightmare of Will's entire reality. She imagined the faces of his visitors. Finally she grabbed her journal and sat on the floor in her bathroom. She leaned against the cabinetry as she rubbed her eyes with one hand and opened her spiral bound book with the other.

Dec. 8, 2009

There's something that happens when your eyes are opened. Something that shifts within your soul. When you lie awake in your bed, with cushy pillows, covers, warmth, and a loyal dog sleeping at your feet, and all you can do is shudder, toss, turn... because you CAN'T FORGET THEM. You don't even know them. You don't know all their names. You just know that they are where they are. And it's not OK. Awareness... Changes you. What do I do with this? I don't know where to go. But I know for sure, I don't want to change back either.

The banquet for the "Colorado Writes" contest was on a Friday a week and a half later. Each author was asked to give a report or overview about their article written. Kayla knew that her article had only touched the surface of what was going on around her, and she wasn't going to focus on the tip of the iceberg. She planned to dig deep.

Her parents and siblings, Josh, and Pete all had place cards at her table. Everyone was dressed up and hundreds of notable community leaders came for the occasion. Exquisite chandeliers sparkled in the ballroom at a hotel in the heart of downtown Denver. Jazz music with a brass ensemble welcomed the crowd. Rex and Regina beamed with pride. While everyone at the table knew that Kayla had been impacted by her relationship with Will, they only thought of him as a poor orphan boy. Only Josh knew how high the stakes were in her life.

The emcee welcomed the crowd; dinner was served

while music played. Kayla's guests around the table conversed in polite chitchat. Pete and Rex hit it off well. Pete was a fun, older character with a wealth of stories and loud sense of humor. Rachel whispered words of encouragement that made Kayla's heart soar, yet as much she wanted to embrace every moment, she couldn't help but worry about Will.

A courteous applause welcomed Kayla as she walked to the stage in the front of the ballroom. She kept her eyes to the floor and tightly gripped the notes and stack of papers in her hand. Her heart beat rapidly as she approached the podium. Looking across the vast ocean of faces, her eyes caught a glance of the cheering squad at her table, all who glowed with huge, encouraging smiles. Josh nodded at her. This was her moment.

"Ever since the first war in the history of humanity, there have been orphans. Ever since the rise of rivalries, the spread of disease, or when hatred and selfishness took root on the earth, orphans have been a part of our stories. Many of these children beg for food or dig in the trash for scraps to eat. Many shiver in the night. All miss their mommy. All miss their daddy. Even if they never knew their biological parents, their hearts desperately long for the safety and security found in their father's arms or mother's whisper. In the United States, there are over 500,000 reported children who are homeless or abandoned.[1] Worldwide there are 153 million orphans.[2] We face a major crisis. Many people have made efforts to help these children, and it will take many more to reach all of them, but there is a special group who have been orphaned in our society."

"These orphans are not just alone, but enslaved by others against their will. These children are the victims of human trafficking. Modern day slavery has become the fastest growing criminal industry in our world today. Sadly, even in our own

1 >> http://www.sos-usa.org/our-impact/childrens-statistics
2 >> http://www.worldorphans.org

country, there is a high demand for child sex exploitation, and there are people willing to pursue their own American Dream at the expense of a child's dignity and safety. These people have stolen the voices of the innocent. Someone must stand in the gap so that the voice of justice can be heard."

"In the United States, it may be difficult to track, but human trafficking happens all around us. Some are forced to work in sweatshops or agricultural fields for grueling 16-hour days with no pay. Others are promised a new life, but become trapped washing dishes, or working in nail salons and massage parlors by day, only to be followed by terrifying nights filled with rape and brutality. These orphans have nearly disappeared on the radar of human compassion. They have become invisible to our society. And as long as this crisis hides in the dark, it will continue, it will get worse, and it will impact all of our lives. I know it has all ready changed mine." She stepped to the side and handed a pile of papers to the emcee across the stage.

"I don't want to leave this place with a simple cheer for decent writing and the façade that we care about these issues. I want to challenge you… to care. So, to equip you in your own journey with this issue, here is a flyer with some resources. Listed you will find organizations who are currently fighting to free these children, and would be so happy to have you join them. I hope that this will not be just another fancy dinner after which we all return to the comfort of our homes and watch "It's a Wonderful Life" on TV. I hope something changes in you. So much has changed in me." She paused for a moment, and her stance grew relaxed as she gave one last personal effort to connect with the audience. "Because the fact is… these orphans, they need someone to love them. And, why shouldn't it be you? Why shouldn't it be me?"

Kayla waited as she looked at the crowd. Some had

tears streaming down their cheeks. Some had their eyes glued to the flyer she had passed out. Others leaned forward with their hands covering their mouth. Her father had his elbows propped on the table and rubbed his forehead back and forth. Josh had a straight face, his eyes beamed with confidence, and he nodded his head again with approving encouragement. After a moment of silence, Josh stood up and clapped loudly. His clapping awakened the room. Few by few, more clapped. Eventually all were standing, and riotous applause filled the room. She didn't smile, she didn't bow; she didn't want this moment to be about her. She just waited. Finally the emcee approached, who also had tears in his eyes. He put a hand on Kayla's shoulder and thanked her.

She stepped off the stage into side wings where others were waiting. Thick black layers of draped curtains cloaked the backstage area in darkness. Kayla could hardly acknowledge the congratulatory remarks of the other authors standing beside her. The last author went up and made a nervous joke about having to follow such a compelling speech. The crowd laughed and enjoyed the opportunity to ease the tension in the room. In just that moment, they had all moved forward, but Kayla could not. Her heart was digging heels into the ground. Where was Will? She stood in the wings as the last person gave his presentation. She did not hear a word of it.

Time stopped when Kayla's cell phone vibrated in her pocket. She had forgotten she had it on her, and it made her jump. Her eyes widened to see an unfamiliar number on the caller ID. The last author finished his presentation and people clapped. The emcee stood up to announce the winner. Moving to the back of the wings near the backstage door, she whispered as she answered the phone.

"Hello?"

"Is this Kayla Barrington?"

"Yes, it is."

"Kayla, this is Jimmy, one of Evan's friend's from CU." Kayla covered her ear with her hand and smashed the phone in her other ear. "I work in the forensics lab for the Denver office."

"Yes, yes, yes."

"Umm. Kayla. The samples that you gave us. They're a match." Kayla's mouth dropped. Her legs tensed. She bent over at the waist and listened intently as her hair fell in her face. "What I'm trying to say is, this DNA, whoever it came from… It's your son."

"Huh?"

"He's your son."

"You're sure?"

"Positive. He's your son."

Kayla started breathing deeply, and faintly heard someone calling her name with the sound of clapping in the background again. She felt hot, she was sweating under her arms, and her stomach was all tingly. The other authors clapped and smiled at her. She heard her name called again. One of her colleagues walked up and pulled her arm toward the light of the stage. She took a few steps while still staring at the cell phone in her hand. The emcee held a crystal trophy in his hands extended toward her.

"I have to find him," Kayla said. The girl pulling her arm looked confused.

"Find who? Come on, this is your moment." Kayla took a few steps back. The applause grew louder as the emcee egged them on.

"She's bashful." He gave a large smile at the audience and then glared back at Kayla. All she could think about was Jimmy's news. *He's your son.* She had been unsure. She had convinced herself otherwise. That was not an option now. Those three words changed her world. The clapping stopped. All was silent.

"This is not my moment. My moment is out there somewhere. I gotta find him," Kayla said. She turned and ran out the backstage door. The metal door slammed behind her, and the cold air outside hit her with a sharp sting. The wind blew steadily, and she heard cars speeding by on the main road. She walked with broad steps in her high heels toward the parking lot. Just a few feet away, she heard the sound of running footsteps behind her. She turned to see Josh chasing after her.

"Kayla! What are you doing?"

"It's a match, Josh."

"What? What is?"

"The DNA. I just got the call. It's a match." Josh put his hands on the back of his head and started pacing back and forth while catching his breath.

"So that means..."

"He's my son."

"What are you going to do?"

"What any mother would do if her baby was stolen. I'm gonna find him."

"How? Wait, what are you gonna do?"

"Honestly, I have no idea. I'm new to this whole mom thing. But I will find him. I will."

The roads were slick. The snow had melted earlier that week, but each night the streets froze over. That night the temperature stayed in the high thirties, so she could hear the sound of slush under her tires as she drove. *Where do I go? Will, where are you?* She knew he wasn't at the Green House. Her mind raced as she remembered all the different places he had mentioned in their conversations. It was a Friday night. It was dark. Her stomach turned, and she hit the gas pedal harder. Will would be exactly where he had told her he had been every night for countless years.

The closest ATM was nearby at one of the major banks. She had not planned her runaway moment in advance. She left her coat at the table, along with a small clutch purse. Her every-day purse was stored underneath the passenger seat of her car. She shivered in front of the ATM and entered the pin and password. She stared blankly at the screen with the blinking cursor.

*How much is it going to cost?* She tapped her fingers on the keypad. *If I find him, can I just pay for an hour? Or the night? Could I smuggle him out if I had a couple of hours? How much? She fixated on the total balance in her account. How much is it going to take?* $1000? $2000? She blinked her eyes and shook her head as she remembered those words. *He's your son.* What wouldn't she pay? She would give it all if she had to. If that's what it took. She would pay any price. This was Will she was searching for. Her Will. And he was worth it.

The ATM maxed out after $400, so she found a slummy "CASH IT NOW" business that was still open. The man behind the counter did not ask any questions. He just grinned as she walked in the door and collected a high percentage on Kayla's transaction. When she returned to her car, she had almost all of her life's savings piled in her fist.

Kayla peered through the fogging windows of her car and drove slowly as she perused the parking lots of different bars and strip clubs. She never saw the fifteen-passenger van, but figured that wouldn't be a great indicator either. She had to go in. Visiting two bars gave no clues, but she was still determined. Even if she had to search every dark hole in the city, she would do it. Down the road was another club. The room was hot, smelled like sweat, and was lowly lit with a few moving colored lights focused on the stage areas. The music was loud and the bass boomed in her heart. The place was packed. The men gave her seductive looks, but Kayla didn't acknowledge anyone until she found the head bartender.

"Lookin' for a job?" he said with a straight face. The bartender was in his late thirties or early forties. His complexion was smooth with a clean-shaven face, but his receding hairline gave his age away. His hair was dark and had a greasy product in it that added a lot of shine. He almost looked like a grease monkey from the 1950s with his hair combed back and his white shirt rolled up at the sleeves.

"Nope." Her throat tightened. "Looking for some fun." She slapped two twenty-dollar bills on the bar. She couldn't tell if her heart was racing because of her own nerves or the dance music vibrating the bar stools. "I'm looking for Will, from the Green House." The bartender looked from side to side, brushed his hands through his greasy hair and bent down close to Kayla. She didn't back away. He eyed her up and down and slowly covered the bills with the palm of his hand.

"Will's a hot commodity." She slammed down four more twenty-dollar bills with a stone face and intense eyes. The bartender smiled and leaned in just a few inches from her face. "E-CLIPSE. Fifty bucks to get in the door. Tell them I sent you." Kayla gritted her teeth, then gave a flirtatious wink with a half smile and a nod as she turned on her heels and headed out the door.

Lower Downtown in Denver was a prime social scene, and E-CLIPSE was known for classy entertainment and an upper class crowd. The interior shimmered with mirrored modern art chandeliers under a romantic blue lighting. Rich dark wood spread across the floor and up the walls as faux columns. Blue velvet bar stools surrounded high top black tables. An attractive woman sang mellow love songs on the stage, and behind her was an illumination of an eclipsing sun and moon. Throughout the room, a smaller eclipsing light with the same image was shining on the walls. Every few minutes the eclipse grew larger, and the sliver of light dwindled.

Men and women in their 30's and 40's filled the room. Most of the men wore trendy suits or business attire with ties loosely hanging around their necks, and the women flaunted cocktail dresses in high heels. Kayla walked to the bar with her eyes to the ground. The drive over could not prepare her for this scene. She shuddered as she glanced at a booth on the side of the club. She remembered eating there with co-workers three years earlier. E-CLIPSE was not the place she could afford to hang out every weekend, but over the years, she received invitations to share drinks for someone's birthday. This was the last place she would have thought to search for Will, and yet here she was. An attractive, thin man served beverages at the bar. He had perfect teeth, a great smile, and noticeably toned upper body underneath his tight black button-up shirt. He had charm, and he knew how to work the crowd.

She took a seat at the bar, and ordered a drink, but didn't touch it. A few minutes later, the light shining on the stage completely eclipsed and booming techno dance music rumbled the floor. People jumped out of their seats and moved quickly to the dance floor. Strobe lights changed the atmosphere of the room as the crowd swayed together. Kayla watched and remembered the hourly ritual. When the song ended, the lights transformed the room back to its classy motif. She slumped as she wondered how close she might have been to her son, and never known.

The bartender served the patrons with a twinkle in his eye. He returned to check on her. She had not touched her glass.

"You don't like it, sweetie?"

"My mind's on other things," she said. She kept her eyes fixed on the bartender and slowly slid a fifty dollar bill across the counter toward him.

"I hear Will is a hot commodity around here."

"Indeed." The bartender gingerly took the cash while walking to the edge of the bar and towards a side door that swung both ways. He flicked his head in her direction and gestured that she follow him.

The music muffled as the door swung shut and she entered a room equally as large as the main dance floor.

"Welcome to E-CLIPSE, phase two." The bartender gave a discreet gesture toward the room. Kayla paused for a moment as her gaze panned the room. The center of the room was filled with cubicles built of the same dark wood used in the other side of the building. The dim glow of large computer screens lit the faces of men and women sitting in each partition. The perimeter of the room had booths with blue velvet curtains drawn for privacy. The light of computer screens peeked through the edge of the fabric.

The bartender was a few steps ahead of Kayla, so she hurried to follow him. A blue curtain flung open and a couple walked out. Hardcore pornography was on the flat screen TV in the booth. As they approached the other side of the room, Kayla saw a black door. A numbered keypad was on the wall to the side of the door. At eye level was the E-CLIPSE logo repeated three times, each with the eclipse progressively covering more of the light. Her leader tapped the buttons on the keypad then opened the door. *Phase Three*, she thought.

She turned down a long hallway with about six shut

doors lined up about ten feet part. Signs over each door read: "Executive Office," along with a piece of paper and handwritten number taped up underneath. As she passed each door she heard the muffled sounds of men and women. The walls were red, the lighting had spotlights aimed at the floor leaving circular shapes in her path. With a hand placed on each front pocket, she felt the bulge of cash, and Kayla's heart broke for her son. She wanted to hold him in her arms, and cry, and apologize, and erase every evil memory from his soul. This hallway had been his childhood playground. She wanted to reverse time, start over, and raise him the way she should have. Her arms tightened. She cracked her knuckles, and the popping sound made the bartender look back at her. His eyes reminded her of the mission at hand. She had to be brave enough to convince the next guy to let her in. Then she had to convince Will to get out.

The bartender brought her to the end of the hallway where two men sat at a small folding table. Cards and cash were in disarray all over the table. Both men were probably in their fifties. One was well over six feet with long legs and silver hair. The other was short with dark curly brown hair and trendy eyeglasses.

"She's here for Will." The two men turned, sizing her up. The shorter one got up and stood toe to toe with Kayla.

"How long you lookin' for? He goes fifteen minutes at a time." Kayla wanted to bend over and violently spit on his white leather shoes.

"The whole night," she said. The men looked at Jay with eyebrows raised.

"Ya know, Will ain't no baby no more. I don't think you'll need the whole…"

"An hour, then."

The short man looked at his watch and noted that most of Will's usual clients had come and gone. The night's rush had passed.

"A special deal for your first time."

Kayla's offer was pure profit, and $100 was all it took. Kayla walked down the hall after the pimp gave her a ticket with a number on it. One hundred bucks for her baby. She couldn't wrap her brain around it. One hundred dollars and anyone could walk through Will's door and rape him countless times. People buy groceries for a hundred dollars, or pay their cell phone bill, or go to Disney World. But buying a person's soul? She took in a deep breath as she stood in front of Will's red door. She hated this door, hidden from everything safe.

With one swift move she whisked the door open and shut it behind her before Will looked in her direction. The room was small. A bare twin bed with a metal frame and an old stained pillow was in the middle of the room. Handcuffs were attached to the metal bars. A wooden chair was in the corner. A dim halogen light in the ceiling was the only thing lighting the room.

Will stood with his back to the door. His left hand rested on the metal footboard. He only wore white sequined pants. His back looked more muscular than she had remembered. She always thought of him as a boy, and now, though he wasn't a man yet, she saw that he was growing up. A key ring and small key dangled from the fingers on his right hand. She looked to see that his left hand was actually cuffed to one of the metal bars on the bed. He kept his head down. They were both silent.

Tears streamed down her cheeks, but she wiped them up. *Be brave,* she thought to herself. *Be brave. This boy needs a hero, not a crybaby*. With a tender touch she took the key and unlocked his handcuffs, then dropped them on the bed.

He looked aside at the cuffs. She was caught off guard by Will's profile, which looked so much like her brother, Ricky. She laid a hand on his bare shoulder, and his muscles tensed. He turned and their eyes locked.

"Will." She could only whisper. He took a step backward, and folded his arms in across his chest. He had seen him bare back at the fights in the city, but this context felt so dirty. He appeared so vulnerable.

"What are you…why…what did you do?"

"Will, I've come for you." Will's anger from the other day clashed with utter humiliation.

"What? You're finally cashing in on two years' worth of Subway? Should've known."

"Will, I've come to… There's something I want to tell you." He folded his arms and leaned against the wall. "I want you to come home with me. Live with me. Be a kid again. Be free. Get a whole new chance at life." The tension in Will's jaw started to relax. He looked to the ground and started tracing shapes on the floor with his toes.

"That's not happening any time soon. It's nice you came all this way. Get to see my office, but I don't think you know how you deep you are in all this."

"I don't really care." Kayla spoke louder with determination. "A mom will do anything to save her son. Anything."

"What did you say?" He stepped toward her and began wildly pointing at her. "You think you know something? You think you own me? You think you're a mom just 'cuz you teach me how to spell and buy me chips every week…" She cut him off as he came nose to nose with her.

"I AM your mother, Will!" Her voice strained. She was still not used to hearing that sentence. "I am. Remember the whole Celia thing? I told you there was more to it. Well, it led me back to my own past. And it led me to you. You." Will shook his head and ran his hands through his hair with confused frustration.

"No, no. Not possible."

"You wanna know where you got your name? Tennessee Williams. I had just read *A Streetcar Named Desire* in high school, and I liked it. Tennessee WILLiams."

"Shut up, just shut up, OK?" Will yelled and waved his arms at her. He sat on the bed and bent over to his knees with his hands running tightly through his hair. He rocked back and forth on the bed before the rage boiled up, then he looked at her with fierce eyes.

"I hate you!" His voice cracked. She stood silent. "You think I'm supposed to be happy that you come and drop this bomb on me? It's better when people come in for tricks because at least I know how to handle that. But this, this is messed up!" He stood looking her in the eyes. "How is it possible that you can be the one person I've ever trusted in my whole life? But then you're the person I have hated my whole life? You think I don't know where I came from? Secrets don't last long in the Green House. I was two when one of the older kids told me I wasn't wanted, and my mom tried to kill me. I didn't really get that, but I feared you. Then I got older, and everyday, Father reminded me that I was worthless. A botched abortion. No one wanted me. No one cared. And every night I sobbed, because something in me wanted to believe you cared, but I knew that you didn't. No one did." Will stood before her, firm in his hatred and bitterness. "I needed you! And you were never there!" Kayla was quiet, and all she could bring forth was a slow whisper.

"I am sorry." She sniffled and wiped her runny nose on her hand. "I am so sorry. I can't begin to…"

"Don't even try."

"Please. Will. All I can say is that...I am here now. I never would have wished this life for you. And to tell you the truth, I did want you back then. I did. And I want you now. I know I can't erase it all, or fix it all." Her lip quivered, and her forehead wrinkled. "But I will give all I have to make it right. I am your mother. You know it, Will. And DNA proves it. And I think something inside of me knew it from the day I met you. As your friend, I love you. And as your mom, I want you to come home." She held still and watched his eyes, but her heart sank when he shook his head, 'no.' Right there before her, a wall in his heart was erected, and it was almost as if it had affected the temperature in the room.

"Go away! You tried to kill me seventeen years ago."

"Fifteen. It was fifteen years ago. September 12, 1994." He looked all the more confused. She winced. It never occurred to her that he didn't even know his true age, or his birthday. His humiliation at her correction flashed into irrational anger.

"Don't ever talk to me again! Don't come near me! You think I can't walk out this door and get you killed? I hate you! I always have! I always will." He stepped forward and forced her backward with his threatening presence. Her back brushed up against the door. "This is your one and only chance to walk outta here alive. So, go!"

She didn't walk, she ran. She heard the voices of the pimps calling after her. At the bar, Jay caught her eye, though she was nothing more than a blur sprinting out of the club. Light rain sprinkled. Her heart pounded. With eyes on the rear-view mirrors, she scoped the bar and parking lot. Two men in black leather jackets walked toward her car.

In haste, she drove over a curb and ran a red light to get

away. She sped down the road and took random turns to make sure no one was following her. After catching her breath, she dialed 9-1-1 and made an anonymous report of sexual favors involving a minor. Maybe she couldn't do anything now, but hopefully the police would arrive in time.

The air was cool, and there was still an inch of brown slush covering the streets. She drove halfway home, but knew she couldn't walk in that door. Even though Will had never set foot in that tiny apartment, now it was his home, too. She couldn't go there. Not yet. So, she redirected her route, and picked up her cell phone.

# CHAPTER ▢ 15
⟩⟩⟩⟩⟩⟩⟩⟩⟩⟩⟩⟩⟩

"YOU know where to find me." When Josh got the call he didn't prod for more information. Kayla choked through her words and hung up the phone as fast as possible. She was broken for all that Will had experienced. She was nauseated at the memory of the rooms in the bar she had just left. Intertwined within these memories was the fear of meeting Josh. Her sense of responsibility for the whole mess felt suffocating. She feared his rejection and the Christian response of "I told you so." Despite these fears, she knew she didn't want to go anywhere else.

Rain poured violently and lightning lit up the sky. Snowstorms were quiet, but for some reason on this December night it was warmer than usual, and it sounded as if the whole earth was torn for her. The glow of the lights from within the church lobby spilled out onto the wet parking lot. She parked the car and saw Josh's silhouette with an umbrella in hand as he waited at the glass doors.

She hopped out of the car and he rushed out toward her with the umbrella over his head. She ran. He ran. She couldn't tell the difference between her tears and the rain. His pace started to slow down but hers only gained speed. With a crash, Kayla collapsed into Josh's arms and laid her face in his chest. The force of her body smacked the umbrella out of his hands, and he slowly placed his arms around her. He didn't ask questions, he didn't pick up the umbrella, which was now upside down, collecting cold water at his feet. He didn't rush her away from the rain. He stood strong, firm. He was a rock, a refuge. Something inside of him was pure, and bigger than himself. She held tightly around his waist and cried in his grip. His arms held her up as she shuddered and tried to catch her breath. This was the first time he had touched her since the day they met when she wandered into the church. At that time, he had laid a hand of encouragement on the shoulder of a fearful stranger. Not much had changed. He loosened his hold and looked down at her.

"Are you OK?" She shook her head 'no,' and picked up the umbrella, which was now heavy with rain. Shaking the water out, she lifted the umbrella up over both their heads.

"Thanks," she said. He nodded as they turned and walked to the front doors of the church.

"The ladies' room is to the right. I'll look around for something warm to cover you up." Kayla spent a few minutes in the restroom to clean up. She rinsed her face, wiped the mascara from under her eyes, and then pulled her hair into a high, messy bun. She exhaled deeply, and realized how tired she was. She emerged from the ladies' room, and found Josh waiting in the lobby. He held two velvet church robes, one was blue and one was bright green. Josh held them up and looked back between her and the robes.

"I wasn't sure which color would be best on you." Kayla couldn't help but laugh.

"Are these yours?"

"They were my dad's. He preached in them all the time."

"So, why do you have them?"

"I guess it's just a comfort thing. When I was a kid, I used to hide in Dad's closet from the nursery ladies. They never saw me past the robes hanging there. Dad would be preaching and I could listen to his voice and make up imaginary games in the darkness of the closet. When Dad passed away, I kept them in the closet in my office. Kinda like he's still here." He looked down at the robes one more time, and pulled up the green one in his hands. "Green looks good on you."

"Oh no. These are your dad's. I don't really think I should…"

"You're soaking wet in the middle of the night. Dad wouldn't withhold his robe from a girl like you."

"He probably wouldn't have liked a girl like me." With that, Josh pulled the robe away from her shoulders and teased her.

"Oh, yeah, that's right. I'm sorry. I forgot. We preachers are holier and better than you common folk. How foolish of me to forget." She turned to see his mischievous glance just as he tossed the robe in her direction, but she couldn't duck fast enough before it smacked her in the face. She wrapped herself in the green canopy.

"I just can't go in there right now." Josh was in the doorway that led to the worship center, and he turned back to her. "That's where it all happened. Procedures and stuff. I just can't go there tonight." A part of her still hated that room and all that its dark corners had brought her way. She sat down on a bench against the wall in the lobby. Josh sat down beside her.

"What happened?" he said. Kayla's eyes welled up with tears.

"He hates me!" The truth in her words stung. Kayla sobbed through the whole story. In her narrative, she took Josh to the ATM and quick cash business, the bars, the back room. She told him her whole speech to Will, but then stopped for a moment as she reached Will's response. Josh leaned forward.

"What did he say?"

"That he's hated me his whole life. He knew everything. He knew about the failed abortion. And he said that I was the one person he trusted, and the one person he hated the most. He said he could have me killed. He just doesn't get it. He couldn't hear me, like everything I said just made things worse. I've lost him, Josh. I've totally lost him. And what's worse is I know what's trapping him, but I can't even help."

"I am so sorry." Josh turned away and propped his forearms on his knees. Tension grew, and he tapped his feet on the tile floor.

"What?" she asked. "What's wrong?"

He shook his head without looking at her.

"Preachers aren't supposed to lie, ya know." He turned toward her slowly with his eyes to the ground. He was troubled, and she had never seen him so undone. "What are you thinking?" she asked.

"It's just that… for years I've cried over these aborted babies. I have spent countless hours praying over the files. Praying for the parents, wherever they might be. Half the time, when Dee Ann says I've gone out to lunch, it's really just that I am down in the basement, heartbroken for all these families." He was quiet for a moment, and they both realized that he had been praying for Kayla long before he ever knew her. "And, I've always wondered… if these children had a voice what would they say? People put words in their mouths all the time. Like 'it would be better this way' or 'they wouldn't want to live in this world', or 'I'm not ready, and I wouldn't be good parent anyway.' I guess people fill in the blanks to make themselves feel better. I don't really blame them. But I always wondered, what would these kids actually say in reply?" He looked up at her red nose and glassy eyes. "I guess now I know."

Kayla sat straight up with her hands in her lap. Josh awkwardly cleared his throat. The rain had stopped and all was silent. In her anger, all she could think to do was escape.

"Wow." She stood and rigidly pulled off the robe.

"Did I say something wrong?"

"Something wrong?" She threw the robe on the bench and grabbed her purse. "No, no, I guess I was just surprised. I mean I shouldn't have been surprised. I've been judged by people and by God before. When I came to this clinic, they were all standing there. The church freaks with posters of dead babies. The shouted and called me a whore. They didn't care how scared I was. I've carried the shame, and I've heard the whole condemnation guilt trip before. I just didn't expect it here. Sitting in a church dressed in a robe with my guard totally down. I just thought that you were..." She stopped before she started crying again. Even though she had just wept in his arms earlier, now she didn't want to appear weak.

"What?" he asked.

"Different! I thought you were different from all the other self-righteous bastards who taught me to hate myself and hate God." Josh stood and took a step closer, he spoke with gentleness.

"Kayla, I am not like them. If you really hate yourself, it's because something inside of you can't separate your heart from this death."

"Don't call it that! It was an abortion. A procedure, my choice. My choice! Nobody died!" Her voice wavered. Josh remained calm, as he looked her in the eyes.

"You're right. He didn't die. You've been given a second chance. This stuff isn't about the past anymore. You've been living in the past for fifteen years. And now you know there is a future. Don't miss it."

"But he hates me." Tears fell down her cheeks.

"Well, apparently you hate you, too, and you've tolerated that for a pretty long time. I am sure you could tolerate him hating you a little while, too. Besides, a lot of teenagers hate their parents anyway." Kayla gave a half smile. "Don't give up on him, Kayla. He doesn't know it yet, but he needs you. And you need him, too. You think it was an accident that you dreamed about this kid for thirteen years before you met him? You think it was a coincidence that you nearly ran him over with your car? You love this kid with your whole heart. There's a reason for all this. A bigger picture. I don't know what it's all about, but like you said, you are *in* this!" She knew he was right, but Will's wounds of rejection were starting to scab over, and she feared she might not recover. She turned, walked across the room with squeaky wet shoes, and stood at the glass doors. She remembered the sign that once hung over the clinic doors. In bold red letters it read, "No Exit by Use of Front Doors. All Patients Must Leave Through Back Doors." She was never the same after leaving the clinic that day. She had been slinking through back doors of shame and heaviness ever since. Maybe Josh was right. Maybe it was time to look forward, to use the front doors.

"Hi, Miss Kayla!" Kayla didn't move or acknowledge the little girl behind her.

"Mattie, I thought you were sleeping. Please go back to my office. I will be there in just a second," Josh spoke with a stern tone. Kayla remained still as she stared out the glass doors. The soft blonde curls peeked around into her peripheral view. Mattie smashed the side of her cheek against the glass door with a giggle as she tried to get Kayla's attention. Mattie's brightly colored pajamas and slippers made for a perfect impromptu outfit with her heavy snow coat on top. Kayla glanced over, and Mattie raised a bright yellow daisy up to her face.

"Here you go!"

"Well, thanks, Mattie. Where'd you get that from?" Kayla's eyes felt heavy and started to sting from all the tears. Her nose was congested, but she tried to sound as normal as possible.

"Over there," Mattie replied pointing to a large arrangement on the welcome station. "They don't need it anymore."

"What do you mean they don't need it anymore?"

"They were for a funeral we had here today," Josh said.

"Oh, that's great," Kayla said with sarcasm.

"I think you're the prettiest lady I know," Mattie's smile beamed. Kayla winced and laughed all at once.

"Did you pay her to say that?" She looked back at Josh who raised his hands in defense.

"My hands are clean. That was all her."

"Sometimes if I'm not sure, this helps me." Mattie extended the flower again. Kayla took it and started spinning the stem in her fingers.

"Sure of what?"

"If he loves you." When Mattie smiled, her eyes sparkled as though she was hiding a bundle of secrets in her heart. *Well, does he? Will he ever love me?* Kayla thought.

"Here, I'll show you!" Mattie giggled as she skipped across the room to the bouquet and picked a fistful of flowers. She returned and pulled Kayla's hand with a burst through the glass doors.

"Quick! Daddy says I can't make messes with my flowers inside. So, I always come out here." Mattie splashed in a puddle before sitting on the curb right in front of the doors. The air was still, the dark sky was quiet. "Look! He loves me. He loves me not. He loves me. He loves me not."

This was obviously a time-tested tradition that the little girl had come to know and love. She was sharing her game with Kayla, and for the first time in fifteen years, Kayla didn't mind playing a childish game with a young girl at her side. She didn't feel threatened by the blonde beauty sitting on a wet curb in her pajamas and slippers. She didn't wonder what her daughter would have looked like, or what the sound of her voice might have been. She didn't have to. Blanche never died on that day in the clinic. The miserable character was born that day only in the heart of Kayla Barrington. The death of her daughter was nothing more than an illusion. None of this erased the pain of losing Will just hours before, but it did give Kayla new eyes for the blessing that was Mattie. Together they picked petals and watched as each yellow leaf swam away in the puddles of fresh rain in the parking lot.

# CHAPTER ☐ 16

NINE days passed after Mattie and Kayla plucked petals in the parking lot of the church. Kayla didn't have the courage to search Will out. She would have defended that she was still new to the whole "mom-thing." She tried to live life as normal, but even with an extra mile added to her jogging routine, and more floor exercises in front of the television, she couldn't get a good night's sleep. No amount of exercise or over-the-counter medications could knock her out at night. As long at the moon was shining in her window, she couldn't stop thinking about Will. She wondered where he was and what he was doing in the middle of that dark world. She wondered if even the moon was bright enough to reach the dark corner of his reality. Each night she cried. She cried loud, and quiet. She hid under the sheets, and covered her face with the pillow. She cried until her bloodshot eyes were puffy and stinging in the morning. And when she thought she couldn't weep anymore, she still did.

The Monday after her search for Will, she went to her

parents' house and sobbed in her daddy's lap. They had left several messages on her cell phone since her enigmatic escape from the banquet. She told them everything. They were stunned, and they cried as they listened to her story. Rex wanted to find Will, but Kayla urged them to wait while she tried to sort things out. Her inquiries to the Denver Police Department indicated that investigations were under way, but no details could be revealed. For the rest of the week, someone from the family called each day. Sometimes she ignored them, and other times she answered, even though she had no news to report.

The victim mentality paralyzed her. Many nights she read all online literature related to human trafficking. She was connected to all this. She didn't ask to be, but she was. In her weakest moments, she cried in bed throughout the night, as though she herself had been raped for nearly fifteen years. Self-pity only dragged her lower.

It had been over a week, and with Christmas around the corner, Kayla was determined to fight the depression. It was a sunny Sunday morning. It had not snowed all week, and the slush had disappeared. The newspaper was laid out on the breakfast table, and she let Jack gnaw on newspapers from the day before. As she sat in the kitchen with uneaten cereal in front of her, she reverted to the joys of her youth. She made a list. Whenever the achiever inside of her cried out, she made a list with doodled boxes along the margin. Joy came from checking off those boxes. Will was not on the list.

Important things like laundry and perusing the movie section at the library were on the list. Organizing her junk drawer in the kitchen and cabinets underneath the sink in the bathroom was also on the list. Last minute Christmas shopping was on the list. No, Will was not on the list. But he still knocked on the door anyway.

Kayla nearly jumped off the chair as the banging rumbled the whole apartment. Jack snarled and protectively barked back.

"Coming! Coming! Jack, quiet. Shh! Jack, good boy. Thank you, Jack." She didn't check the peephole since she was more concerned about calming the dog so the neighbors wouldn't complain. She flung the door open and gasped at the sight of Will standing on her doorstep. He wore a white V-neck undershirt, coupled with bleached torn jeans and his Broncos jacket. A tattered navy backpack was at his feet on the ground. His silky brown hair curled around his ears and fell over his forehead. Though his hands were shoved in his pockets, the tone in his voice was anything but relaxed.

"Why didn't you come?" He shouted with a wounded whimper in his tone.

"Come where?"

"Where have you been?" Will sounded like the last kid picked up from school.

"Here. I've been- well, how'd you..." Kayla started rubbing her forehead. Tension grew in her neck and shoulders. She took a deep breath. "How'd you find this place?"

"A dog always knows his way home, right?"

"Right. What? What do you mean?"

"Where have you been?" His anger turned to a desperate plea.

"I was giving you some space."

"Space? I've had space for fifteen years. I don't need space! I've had plenty of space!" Will raised his voice.

"OK, I get it. What are you trying to say?" Will scuffed his feet on the steps and lost his gusto. He tilted his head and combed his brown locks with his hands.

"I just... well, what you said about me... staying here. I

just thought, umm." Kayla waited as the boy paused to find his words. "I'd rather have a mom, even if only for a day, than be an orphan my whole life." He looked up at her. He had new eyes compared to the last time she had seen him. He was vulnerable, unguarded, and hopeful. He took a gamble, and laid everything out on the table. "So maybe we could try this."

The music in her heart swelled and Kayla leapt from the stoop in the front door and embraced her son. She squeezed him tightly, and her feet pitter-pattered an uncontainable happy dance. She pulled away and looked him in the eyes again. He smiled back. She hugged him again. He embraced her and they hopped and danced on the porch. All she could say was "Yes!" over and over again with an occasional "Thank you" as well. Jack sat at the front door, and nudged his nose close enough to lick her leg. She stepped back to the doorway of the apartment and lifted her hands up in the air with a great exclamation.

"Welcome home, Will! Come inside!" She looked down at Jack and introduced the two of them as well. Will smiled and rubbed Jack's soft and floppy ears while the dog covered him in slobbery kisses. Kayla skipped about the apartment and gave Will an official tour.

"This is your kitchen, and this is your TV. Back here is your desk, and your bathroom is through that door." Will laughed at her presentation.

"I just scored the jackpot!" he said.

"We are a family now. What's mine is yours."

There was no other day like this day for both Will and Kayla. It was like the excitement of a wedding day, or a new baby being born. Will had not eaten in nearly three days, so Kayla made him several heaping plates of chocolate chip pancakes with eggs, and bacon, all doused in syrup. She wiped her happy tears as she stirred the eggs on the stove. Shortly after breakfast, Kayla's eyes lit up across the table.

"Let's go shopping! Come on! Let's go!" She grabbed his hand and pulled Will him to the car. She took Will to the mall, and bought him new jeans, new shirts, a new pair of shoes and lots of socks and underwear. She held clothing up to him to check his size and then sent him into the dressing room with a fresh armful of things. He never asked for anything, which made her want to give all the more. She ripped the tags off of a few of her favorites and brought those with a pile of others to the counter. She wasn't about to have him leave in the filthy rags he had walked in wearing.

The rest of the day was spent relaxing. Will look a three-hour nap on her bed. She covered him with a blanket, and made hot tea in the next room. She was exhausted by the emotional roller coaster over the past few weeks, but then something inside her still wanted to get up and dance. She thought of the boy in her room, and all she could do was smile.

While Will slept the afternoon away, Kayla made phone calls to her family and announced the news that Will had come home. Josh was ecstatic, and Mattie cheered in the background. Regina cried, and Rex thanked God every other minute. They wanted to drive right over, or at the very least have Kayla and Will over for dinner that night, but Kayla wanted to have her first dinner with just the two of them. Respectfully, they understood, but she promised to be at dinner with the whole family the next night on Christmas Eve. Will came out of the bedroom rubbing his eyes.

"Are you up for one more field trip and then I promise we can veg out and relax all night?"

"Sure," he said.

It was a tradition that her parents had created for their family. When she pulled up to the King Soopers grocery store with Christmas trees lined up against the outside, Will jumped out of the car with a huge smile.

"I've never had a Christmas tree before," Will said as he zipped his jacket.

"Never?"

"Other houses had them, a bunch would set the tree up so you could see it out their front window. I used to stare at those trees, back when I was little. I loved them. Celia and I'd walk past the house over and over again just to watch the tree."

"Well, take your pick." Kayla gestured toward the trees. They both planted their cheeks in the evergreen branches and smelled the timeless fragrance. With only two days until Christmas, there wasn't a huge selection of trees, but to Will and Kayla there could have been no greater memory than this. Once they chose an eight-footer with full branches, the grocery staff helped tie the tree to her car. Kayla ran inside to grab a few things. She figured some candy canes, popcorn, and cranberries would work for decorations. As she returned to the car, Will and the stock boy fastened the tree atop her tiny car.

"Can you take a picture of us with our tree?" She handed the employee her camera from the back seat. The boy snapped a shot capturing an incredible moment for this little family. They stood in front of the car with the green Christmas tree tied on the roof. Will put his arm around her shoulder and they both smiled. Shoppers rushed by with their carts full of groceries. None would have imagined the story right in front of them.

That night Kayla and Will dressed their Christmas tree in lights along with strings of popcorn and cranberries. Will was the greatest gift she had ever gotten for Christmas. They ate an eclectic dinner of corn dogs in the oven, along with chips and salsa, and hot cocoa. The little apartment glowed with the twinkle of their tree, and Christmas movies played in the background as they talked the night away. Kayla insisted that she sleep on the couch so that Will could rest under her soft duvet. Will was courteous, but eventually gave in and took the bedroom. He was in bed when she tiptoed into the dark room. She sat on the edge of the bed and stroked the hair on his forehead just as her mother had done for her so many times. A sliver of light peeked through the bathroom door and illumined the bed. Will closed his eyes, as she stroked his face.

"I love you," she whispered. He simply nodded with his eyes closed.

Her heart was so full she thought it might burst, and this was only the first day.

Kayla had hoped for sweet dreams, the kind of visions that make no sense in any realm but a dream world. She had hoped to fly above the clouds, and dance in bright colored dresses, or ride upon dolphins in a silver sea. The kind of dreams that make you laugh in your sleep, or leave you smiling when you wake up. Instead she woke up with knots in her stomach. She could not remember the scenes from the night before, but there were faces fresh on her mind as she got up for breakfast. Kayla flipped pancakes for Will, and all she could think about were the other children stuck in the Green House. She was quiet that morning, and so was Will. She wondered if he had the same dreams she did. She knew it was the right thing when she saw the smile on Will's face.

"We have to get them." She sat down at the kitchen table with a plate full of pancakes. Will's cheeks bulged with his breakfast. He placed his force on the table and swallowed.

"Really?"

"They were your family, we can't leave them in that hell-hole. We need to call the police and figure out the next steps," she said.

"No, no, wait. No cops. We just gotta go in fast and get out."

"Will, it's too dangerous. This is the only way."

"Nope. Not the only way. When you called the cops on E-CLIPSE, nobody was rescued. Everybody just moved to a new spot. I can take you to the kids. The boss will be out all day doing drugs. Plus, I didn't come back yesterday, so you know they are on edge. There's no time to waste."

"This is insane."

"We have to do it! Nobody else will ever find them. They'll be gone forever. Please!"

Kayla recruited the help of her dad, both brothers, and her brother-in-law. They all drove to Kayla's apartment where they mapped out a plan. Kayla took great joy in introducing Will to his grandfather. Rex gave Will a great big hug, and called him "son" a couple of times. Will sat close to Rex on the couch. She could tell that he was starved for a healthy relationship with a dad.

"How many?" Rex asked. Will counted silently on his fingers.

"Nineteen of us. Well, that was before..." Will looked down remembering Celia.

"So, eighteen, including Will," she said. "Plus five drivers. So we should be able to fit in three cars plus your van, Dad. It will be tight, but the fewer cars the better. "

"We gotta be quiet and fast." Will briefed the group on the location. "Boss won't be there. Mother's always hung over in the bedroom. Everybody 'round there is no good. They all stick together. You gotta wear a hat, keep your face down. Be invisible."

Will put on his old clothes so as not to distract the kids. Everyone dressed in jeans, dark colors, and wore hats. Kayla took deep breaths and popped her knuckles. She was terrified, and she didn't want to take Will back there. She didn't want to lose him again. All she could do was pray one word: "Help."

They parked across the street on the side of the motel farthest from the manager's office. She leaned her head to the steering wheel and texted Josh: "Please pray. We are here." He responded: "You can do this." In one phone call, the plan was put into motion.

"9-1-1, what is your emergency?"

"I would like to report a case of human trafficking."

"Of what, ma'am?"

"Children. Who have been kidnapped, raped, held against their will. We need the police to come right away." Kayla proceeded with the address and physical description of the Father and Mother before hanging up the phone.

Only Will, Kayla and Rex went on site. The others waited in the car so that they could help the children in the escape vehicles. The motel looked nearly empty. Not much movement. They crossed the street, and Will pointed to a lookout place for Rex to wait around the corner. Rex held a hunting rifle underneath his long jacket. The motel room was around a corner; Will and Kayla tiptoed in silence. Will cracked the door slowly. Half of the kids slept in a pile on top of one another. Others ripped apart old Playboy magazines to make paper airplanes. Catch was sprawled on the floor with a bulging black eye. Will squatted low to the ground and snapped his fingers at the children. He spoke in a whisper.

"Listen. It's time for us to go. Trust me, OK?" The children nodded. "You gotta stay real quiet, and come with my friend."

Kayla walked one child at a time to her dad who put his arm around their shoulder, covered their face, and walked them across the street to one of the cars. Will crawled on his belly across the floor to the children still asleep. Kayla kept count as she walked each child down the shadowed hallway. It had only been about six minutes and nearly all the children were buckled up in the cars. Fourteen. Fifteen. Sixteen. She looked across the room. It was empty. Who was missing? She and Will looked at one another and their minds raced as they tried to remember each child who had been rescued. Will crawled behind the couch to look around the corner. He was out of sight when May popped out of the bathroom door. Her little voice was giddy and unrestrained.

"Look, Miss Kayla! Hippo had to go potty before his long trip!" May held the teal hippo that Kayla had given in her arms. Kayla squatted down on the floor and covered her lips with her pointer finger. But May didn't look at Kayla. Her eyes fixated high, and tears welled up as her bottom lip quivered. Kayla felt the cold barrel of a gun rest on the back of her neck. Her back arched and she instinctively raised her hands above her head as she slowly stood up with the guiding nudge of the gun.

"Where are they?" The Father's voice grumbled in fury.
"Who?"
"Don't lie to me! These kids aren't worth your life, but I will kill you if I have to."
"I don't know what you're talking about," she said. The gun pushed harder into her neck and Kayla cringed with squinted eyes. Slowly Will stood up from behind the sofa. His hands were in fists, and he held his chin low like he was ready to jump into the alley fight club.

"Well, well, well. We missed you last night, Will. Nice of you to come home."

"This is not home." Will's eyes burned with rage.

"This is all there is!"

"No! Not for me. Or any of these kids. Nobody. We are done with this." He smirked at Will's audacity. The Father clicked the safety lock off the gun pointed at Kayla's head. She winced. Help, she prayed. If you can hear me, please help!

"You really think you can come in with a stupid little girl like this and beat me? I own you, and I didn't last this long by being stupid!" The Father's voice grew wilder, and she could feel the gun shaking behind her. "Now, tell me where all the brats are before I shoot you, and May, and your little girlfriend here. Don't test me, Will!" The gun shook erratically as the evil voice grew louder.

Suddenly, Kayla heard a loud metal-like clunk and she screamed as she saw the Father slump to her side. His gun slid across the floor hitting the edge of the couch. Her dad stood over the two of them. His rifle was still raised from the dense blow against the Father's head. His hands quivered in the tight grip of the gun.

"Come on. Let's go!" Rex urged them out the door. Will scooped up May in his arms. Rex grabbed Kayla's hand to run, but she nearly fell on her face when tripped by the grip of the Father's hand. He cursed and pulled her back, but Rex would not let go. At the same time, the Father regained reach of his gun as Kayla kicked enough to release her predator's clutch-es. He shot loosely and hit the doorframe. Will and May were nearly across the street by the time Rex and Kayla turned the corner. The sound of gunshots echoed throughout the street, and Kayla ducked for cover while running to the cars. Rex held her hand tightly as they raced for safety. She looked back to see the Father stumbling in the hallway. He rubbed his head, and shot aimlessly in their direction. The tires screeched as the cars peeled out of the area. The Father ran to the middle of the street screaming wildly and emptied his gun at the cars which were now long gone. In her rear view mirror, Kayla saw the flashing lights of police cars arriving at the scene as the Father made a mad dash toward the motel. The muffled sirens disappeared as they drove off.

The cars sped in different directions. Each car took a separate route home and once certain they were not being followed, all reported to a local Walgreens just a few blocks from Rex's house. No one cheered, or spoke. They could hardly breathe. Everyone looked out the window with silent hope of freedom. When all of the vehicles arrived at the Walgreens parking lot Kayla took a head count.

"Fifteen, sixteen…" She looked down at May standing next to Will. "Seventeen," She placed a hand on May's head.

"Don't forget Hippo!" May stretched the toy up above her head. Kayla smiled with tears in her eyes.

"Eighteen." She tapped Hippo's nose. Kayla picked May up and she wrapped her legs tightly around Kayla's waist. "OK," Kayla bent down to look them in the eyes. "Time for dinner! Back in the car. We can't be late." The children chattered with excitement as they tried to guess where they would be eating.

Regina waited at the front porch wearing a Christmas apron. She waved a hand at them as the cars pulled into the driveway. Regina and Rachel warmly greeted every child with hugs as they tumbled out of the cars. Their tears washed the dirty cheeks of the little ones as they swayed and danced with each one on the front lawn. Kayla opened the front door and ushered the children inside. The house smelled of warm cookies, and a live evergreen tree. Aromatic whiffs from the kitchen made the children salivate. They planted their faces on the outside of the oven to see the food that cooked inside. The children danced and cheered in amazement, all to the beat of Christmas tunes playing in the background.

Two caseworkers from the police department sat at the kitchen table. Typically, the children should have been processed through the social services system, but Pete Rivers used some professional connections for Kayla to allow an exception for this situation. The caseworkers gently took one child at a time to a spare bedroom to take photos, personal information, and swab for D.N.A. Will stayed with each child. Earlier that afternoon, Regina had bought red and green sweat suits for each child. As they changed, their original clothing was bagged for processing as evidence. The caseworkers wore civilian clothing and jotted notes for the report throughout the night. An officer's detail was assigned to watch the Barrington's street for any suspicious activity.

The whole family circled up, joined hands, and Rex said a prayer of thanks for the children rescued. Some of them looked up in surprise by the honoring words Rex used about them. The children sat in chairs throughout the kitchen and dining room as they ate dinner. The adults stood around them, ate with plates in hand, and served more food whenever asked. The house was full, and it had never been so wonderful. In the midst of the happy chaos, Regina and each of the other family members gave Will a special greeting and welcome to the family. Kayla stole away for a moment to text Josh: "We made it. All are safe. Merry Christmas."

She looked up to the sound of a jolly "Ho Ho Ho!" Coming down the stairs was her dad dressed in a red Santa suit. She looked to her mom who gave a knowing wink. Santa brought presents of candy, crayons, Nerf guns, soccer and basketballs, Barbie Dolls, and Polly Pockets. Each child squealed with glee. Kayla wiped her tears as she watched her daddy hand out gifts while trying to maintain the pillow shoved in his red coat. The children piled in sleeping bags with pillows and blankets all in the family room by the warm fireplace. Finally the house grew quiet. The caseworkers from the police department slept on the couch in the formal living room. The Christmas tree, in full splendor, served as a night light over the children.

# CHAPTER □ 17

THE upcoming spring months in Denver brought a season of healing for Kayla and Will. For the sake of safety and giving more space for her son, they moved in with her parents. Will stayed in Ricky's old room, and Kayla moved her queen bed into her room. In the past, she might have been anxious over the memories from that room, but with a little prayer, and a lot of redecorating, Kayla felt more at home there than she had anywhere else in the past fifteen years. She was starting over.

After Christmas, Kayla worked with the Family Services Office to find homes to adopt the children she had rescued from the Green House. They were currently living in foster homes and received daily visits from a clinical psychologist. Twice a week the children came together for a supervised evening at Kayla's house. The culture shock of being separated was difficult for them, and the visits to the Barrington home was helpful in their recovery. In less than two months, all of the children were welcomed into loving homes. Many of the new parents were from Josh's church and volunteered through the Foster Care System. It would have been most difficult to say goodbye to May, except that it was Kayla's sister, Rachel, who gave her a new home. Kayla watched May jump on her new bed and play in the yard with her new siblings. She had not realized it, but even Rachel's family had been dramatically changed by these children. Everyone was.

Will seemed happier than ever, though hard days did wander through. Josh and Rex helped Will in the moments that he recoiled in fear. On occasion his insecurity from the past would metabolize into unleashed anger, but with Josh's counsel, the family continued to surround him with love.

"Years of wounds will not heal overnight," Josh said.

"I'm just sick of having people look at me weird. I want it all to be over!" Will raised his voice.

"Take it one day at a time. We are here for you."

"Will, nobody looks at you weird. No one knows your past. Your whole life you walked around and no one knew you were trapped. They can't see it now either," Kayla said.

"Why can't I see Catch?"

"Give him some time. Everyone is adjusting," Josh said.

At night Kayla tucked Will in and reminded him of how much she loved him. Sometimes her tears fell over his covers while she caught up on the years of lullabies and pep talks she had missed out on. She could tell that he was struggling when she told him she loved him and heard no response. If he didn't answer, she would just brush the hair out of his eyes and whisper, "Remember, your mama always loves you. Always." But most nights her heart would leap at her son's sweet words.

"Love you, Will."

"More." He nodded with eyes shut and a content smile.

"Nope."

Will and Catch played basketball in the driveway with Rex or one of Kayla's brothers. Catch also had issues to deal with, and a family from Church on the Rock walked through it with him. His new parents also gave Catch a new name.

"They said that Peter was tough, and passionate, and always got his foot stuck in his mouth." Catch dribbled the ball.

"Then that's perfect!" Will said with his eyes on the ball.

"Yeah, but they said that Peter also turned out pretty cool. He wasn't afraid of nothing."

"Well, it might take a while for me to get used to." Will stole the ball and dribbled between his legs. "But I don't care what I call you as long as I still have someone to beat at basketball!" Peter accepted the challenge and the boys played ball until the sun went down.

As routines were developed, the Barrington family grew closer. Will wanted to keep his first name, but took on Kayla's maiden name.

"No more Will Green," he said. Kayla pictured all the children who, over the years, found their identity in the Green House.

"Welcome to the family," she said with a smile.

Kayla still worked at the Denver Post doing the same jobs she had done before. From time to time, Pete Rivers assigned a writers challenge with a twinkle in his eye and a glance in her direction. Sometimes, though, Pete was not so subtle with his assignments. On the day after Christmas, he invited Kayla back into his office. He listened to the flood of adventures she had experienced over the past week. He smiled when he heard the children were safe and Will was home.

"This is your story, Kayla." Pete leaned forward in his chair. Kayla could not help but notice he called her by her first name. "I'm not trying to exploit your family here, but you have to write about this, about this slavery thing."

"I don't know."

"Barrington, you are passionate about this. Your heart is raw and bleeding for this issue. Your voice speaks with experience. Give me 1000 words by Friday," he said with a slam of his hand on the desk.

"Boss, are you crazy?" He looked up at her bold response.

"Not crazy. I want those words on my desk before you leave the office on Friday."

"Yes, sir."

The next two days Kayla worked around the clock pulling together research surrounding human trafficking while weaving in her personal story. She interviewed Will for details from his past. When she asked him if it was OK to share bits of the story, he agreed. She kept all of the names anonymous, but gave enough details to prove to the public that this was not a fairytale or piece of horror fiction. Kayla was also surprised to see a dozen copies of the Denver Post sitting on her chair on the morning of New Year's Eve. The front page, in bold print read: CHILDREN OF THE CITY, and her byline was beneath it. Co-workers congratulated her, and Evan offered to pick up her usual Starbuck's order that day. The family and children all cheered when she came home with an arm full of papers.

Though there was not a whole lot of snow in those early spring months, it felt as though so much of Kayla's heart was gently being washed clean. Kayla continued to help Will with his schoolwork, and enrolled him in a home school program. Regina taught classes for both Will and Peter, and a few of the other children who lived close by. Kayla still treated Will to Subway each week, and she laughed as he marveled at the cleaner restaurant with updated décor just around the corner from their house. This was a tradition that she didn't want to forgo even with the new schedule in their lives.

She, Will, and Jack enjoyed early morning runs around the neighborhood each day. Though she had been jogging for years, Will, in his young, fit physique kept her huffing and puffing and pushed her harder each week. Will kept treats in his pocket for the black Labrador and teased that the two of them would leave Kayla behind if she couldn't keep up.

"What's wrong?" Will asked. Kayla sat on the back porch of the house staring at a yard full of children playing. The sun sat on the edge of the mountain horizon. Six weeks had passed and Kayla welcomed all the former Green House kids over for dinner on Valentine's Day. The recent days had received mild temperatures and the kids enjoyed the fresh air outside. Rachel brought May and the older siblings helped lead games for all the children. Their laughter was infectious, and Kayla sat in awe by their resilience. Just six weeks earlier, these children were living every day in the darkness of slavery. Now they ran in the grass together, making up imaginary games.

Peter had not been able to make it. Lately, he was having trouble at home. The family took him to counseling for depression and feared he might wander off into the wrong crowd. While he was grateful for his new home, the process of restoration was not effortless. Kayla knew that Will missed his friend, and her heart weighed heavy.

"Oh nothing. I am fine," she said.

"So, how many times do I have to ask you before you start telling me the truth?" Will said. This had actually been a phrase that Kayla used on her son whenever he was having a rough day.

This new mom had noticed many unexpected magical moments with her son over the past months. Just as a toddler might experience something for the first time with bright eyes full of wonder, Kayla had come to recognize that expression on Will's face as well. She loved this part of motherhood more than anything.

As a teenager, Will didn't resent his ignorance of a particular subject or mope at the thought that he had missed out on life. Just as a baby relishes a new taste, or laughs when knowledge becomes plainly obvious, Will welcomed each day with expectation. He had never eaten cornbread with chili on a rainy day. He had never been asked which movie he wanted to watch. Choices were never a normalcy. He had never read a thrilling story and longed for the heroic ending, or taken a walk as the sun set slowly in the horizon. And he had absolutely no concept of Valentine's Day. Never had he been given a card. He remembered that one time Celia came home with a rose, but the Father tore it to pieces in front of the other children. Celia cried the entire morning while the rest of the house slept.

On this day, Kayla peeked out her door and watched Will's surprise when he nearly crushed a big heart-shaped box of chocolates placed on the floor outside his room. Now she sat watching the yard full of children, and she ached knowing that so many of those precious moments were lost.

"I hate how much I lost with you." Will looked away as she continued. "Years. Years of Valentine's Days. Years of memories. Years that I should have been protecting you." She gestured out to the crowd of kids in her backyard. "Years of seeing you at this precious age. I never get that back." The two sat silently as the sun suspended in the sky for their moment together.

"I remember the day I met you. What son can say that about his mom?" He smiled. "Maybe we just figured this whole thing out now, but I have had almost two years with you. Lunches, homework, Christmas, the Broncos. I would go to bed with you on my mind." She finally looked at him and saw tears in his eyes. "You gave me hope. I never had that before." He grabbed her hand and looked out to the kids at play. "And if you had me then, where would they be now?" Chills rose up and down Kayla's spine as she admired the unreasonable wisdom in her son. "I have you now." Will was now just a tad taller than Kayla and he put his arm over her shoulder. They stood together for only a moment before the beckoning calls of the children invited them to join in the games.

Kayla's favorite part of the week was Thursday nights in the kitchen. Most nights Regina cooked and Will or Kayla helped, but on Thursdays, Kayla was responsible for whatever ended up on the table. She and Will were a great team. They grooved in their favorite Converse All Stars to the beat of loud music. She and Will tried new recipes. Sometimes their efforts were failures, but most of the time the kitchen sizzled with the sounds of fresh veggies cooking in the skillet and the awakening aroma of mixed herbs and spices.

On this night, the meal was open to anyone who wanted to join in for supper. Sometimes Peter stopped by, or Rachel and the kids. Ricky was almost always there, and on occasion Josh and Mattie would walk through the door as well. Over the months, the table had featured a span from meat loaf, to Hawaiian chicken, southern sweet corn with pork, or homemade lasagna. Kayla's desserts were a top-secret project. If anyone showed up early, she kicked them out of the kitchen so she and Will could prepare the finishing touches. People put in requests for her pineapple upside down cake, or banana soufflé, or crunchy caramel apple cobbler. She loved cooking, and since she only did it once a week, it became a special event. The time with Will was priceless as they talked, and sang, and danced across the tile floor with spatulas in their hand.

On this particular Thursday in late April, the sun was shining, and the weather was crisp, but Kayla felt deflated after a long day at work. The busy day had gotten the best of her. She dropped her purse and a few work files on the kitchen table, and then sighed as she slouched in a chair and played with some fruit in a bowl on the table. Her mom vacuumed upstairs. Dad would be home soon, hungry as always. She heard Will's footsteps jumping down the stairs. He snapped his fingers and shuffled across the room then turned some music on in the kitchen. Pieces of different lyrics skipped as he searched for the right song. Soon she heard the beat to a familiar favorite, and smiled as she rested her head on the table.

"I got sunshine… on a cloudy day," Will sang as he snapped his fingers and stepped in smooth rhythm. Kayla kept her head down, but giggled a bit as she saw Will's dramatic karaoke moment in the kitchen. "When it's cold outside… I got the month of May."

"It's still April, ya know," she said. Will grabbed her hand and pulled her onto the makeshift dance floor between the table and kitchen island.

"Well, I guess you'd say: 'What can make me feel this way?' My girl. My girl. My girl." He spun her around and sang in a silly high voice. "I used to sing this to Celia all the time," he said. Kayla winced at the thought of Celia. "I'm glad I have you," he said with a smile. After a minute he caught on to her mood and his dance moves slowed to a stop. "Are you OK?"

"Yeah, sorry. Just a rough day at work." she said.

"You're ready for stir fry, right?"

"Yeah, actually, I think I'm gonna jog for like fifteen minutes to clear my head."

"You want me to come?"

"No, that's cool. I think I want some fresh air and a few minutes to recoup, ya know." She headed back toward the foyer and up the stairs. "I seriously won't be longer than like ten or fifteen minutes. You wanna just start chopping stuff up?"

"Sure thing," he said as he pulled out the cutting board. "Be back in a few minutes."

Even just changing clothes and feeling her running shoes on her feet started to bring back some perspective. Jack whined at the front door, but she left him behind. As she jogged down the sidewalk she noticed an unfamiliar old car parked a few houses down across the street. She ran in the opposite direction. Her pace was slower, and her feet felt heavy. The sunlight was glowing softly over the mountain range. With a deep exhale, she picked up the pace and listened to the chirping of the birds in the surrounding green trees. She smiled thinking of Will and his sweet serenade.

A loud gunshot cracked through the air. She stumbled with a jolt of surprise. A flock of birds flew away from the direction of her house. Like a start whistle in a race, Jack's vicious barking sent Kayla sprinting back home. The sound of her mother's scream sent nauseating heat flashes through her body. Desperate panic blasted like lightning through her veins which propelled her forward. As she darted across the front yard, she saw Will's feet lying on the floor just inside the foyer with the front door wide open.

Fleeing from the house was a middle-aged man in black

boots and military green canvas coat. In his hand was the same gun that had once been pointed at her head. She screamed in rage as the Father turned his face in her direction. Still running to his car he twisted his torso and shot in her direction. She ducked moving toward the front door steps. Indecision tore her between two destinations. A small pool of dark blood to the side of Will's torso caught her eye. She spun around quickly as she heard a car door slam. Nearly knocking her over was her dad running through the yard with his own rifle in hand.

"Daddy!" She screamed as the Father's car peeled out in the escape. Rex shot at the car. The back window shattered. One of the back tires blew out, but the car continued on. Rex kept running after the car while yelling vengefully. Kayla's feet tripped as she stumbled to the front door.

There he was. Her son gasped for breath on the floor. He gripped his torso tightly and blood spilled between his fingers. Regina was in the kitchen on the cordless phone hysterically trying to report the attack. Her heart raced as she tried to take in the situation. A few chopped vegetables lay on the cutting board with the knife beside them. Kayla fell to her knees.

"Oh, God! Oh, God, please, no! Will? Will, can you hear me?" He nodded slowly and his eyes bulged in desperation as he looked up at her. She choked as if drowning in her son's blood. Will gasped for air, and his jaw shook as his teeth clenched tightly. She pulled his head up in her lap.

"Mom, bring some towels!" Regina ran over with towels in one hand and the cordless phone in the other. "Pressure, put pressure here!" Regina quickly moved Will's hand and more blood spilled out from the wound. She put the phone down and held the towels on Will's side with both hands. Heavy footsteps pounded up to the front door as Rex returned.

"Is help coming?" Regina nodded to her husband. Rex

got down on all fours in Will's face. "Don't worry, Will! You're gonna be OK. Help is coming." Rex moved in nervous, clumsy motions. He stood up and looked out the front door, running his hands through his hair. He hit his fist on the doorframe and watched down the street. Kayla just kept her gaze on her son. His shoulders were propped in her lap, and she supported his head with one arm and tightly gripped his hand. He was struggling, but she felt a lingering strength in his hands.

"You can do this, Will. Just hold on, please, sweetie. You can do this," she said. Will moved his mouth to speak, but no sound came out. She leaned in close with tears pouring down her cheeks. His strength cracked, but he continued in a whisper. She smiled through her sobs as she heard the slow, shaky serenade.

"I got... sunshine...on a c-cloudy day... I guess..." Will's energy faltered and his eyes started to roll a bit. He gasped for air and grunted in pain. Looking back up again, their eyes met, and he gave a faint smile in a violent exhale. "My girl. My girl." He grew weaker and his body quivered. She gently shushed him in her arms.

"Shh, Shhh. Just rest. Save your energy." She looked into his eyes. Her parents were quiet. All was quiet. Only the sound of her shrill gasps as she tried to catch her breath. She hugged him tightly and rocked him slowly. She could feel his pulse through the veins in his neck. "I love you so much, Will." All she could do was sob through her words. "You have changed my life. You know that, right? I needed you all along. The whole time." She hugged him again and whispered in his ear while her tears washed both their cheeks. "I need you now. Please don't go. I love you so much. You know that, right?" She felt his head slowly nod "yes" against her cheek.

"I know, Mom," he whispered. She rocked. She hummed

in his ear. And in those still moments, she sang. She sang just as a mama sings her baby to sleep.

"You are my sunshine, my only sunshine. You make me happy…" and then she felt his hands loosen. His head dropped in her arm. And he was gone.

The police and rescue units heard Kayla's loud, broken cries from the car as they arrived. Daylight had turned to dusk, and the glow spilling out of the open front door created a silhouette of a mother rocking her dead son in her arms. Rex sat on the porch steps in quiet tears. Regina held the wound with her head down on Will's stomach. And Kayla just gripped tighter, compensating for her son's lifeless body.

# CHAPTER □ 18

THIS was worse than the first time Will died. Maybe because something in the depths of her heart knew he was still alive. Now there was no doubt. She had seen it, felt it, and experienced it herself. When the police arrived, she did not move. She held him for another 30 minutes. A few officers waited at the kitchen table while the others trailed the Father. A helicopter flew over the surrounding neighborhoods. Regina returned to the kitchen sink and used a sponge to wipe blood off of the portable phone. She looked to the left of the sink and saw the cutting board with chopped vegetables. She lifted it to dump in the trash.

"No! Please!" Kayla left her son and ran to the sink. She pulled the cutting board out of her mom's hands, and the vegetables tumbled to the floor. She cried as she knelt to the floor. She trembled as she swept the mess with her hands. "That's our dinner. He's making me dinner." Kayla dumped the food back on the cutting board, and meticulously moved each piece back. She leaned her face close over the counter, still fidgeting with the vegetables. "I just left for a minute. He was getting it started for me. 'Be right back.' I was coming right back." Regina placed her arms around Kayla from behind, and laid her cheek on her daughter's back. The officers remained quiet with their gaze down in their laps.

There were no words. Silence immediately became her lonely friend. When she washed the blood off her face and hands in the solitude of the bathroom a shroud covered her heart. She could hardly focus during the experience of crime scene investigations and preparations for the funeral.

Her family surrounded her with support. Dee Ann and others from the church brought flowers and food every day for several weeks. Josh was the most faithful of friends, yet she still felt completely alone. She could not eat, or hardly talk. She could not write. She held a pen in her hand, but it was as if her arm had been cut off and could not move it over the pages in her journal. Everything felt numb. At times she felt as though God was talking to her, but she ignored him. Other times she was sure God was weeping with her. So she joined him in tears.

The Father and Mother were caught within hours of the attack. Investigators suggested that Will was targeted to silence those still enslaved. If word got out that a teenager stood up to the oppressors, it might cause an uprising. The policeman said that the news of the arrest might help bring some closure. It was surreal as the officer spoke of such an absurd notion. Closure. She wanted to lash out, but sat silent, in awe of the full circle in which she had come.

She didn't have the courage to speak to anyone, but knew she had to tell Peter face to face. She drove to his house the next morning.

"What? Are you kidding?"

"No, I'm not. The Father came to our house. I was out

jogging and Will answered the door," Kayla said. They sat together on the couch in his new home. His adopted parents stood in the doorway. Kayla put one hand on his back, and wiped her tears with the other.

"Naw, naw. I don't get it. Not like this."

"I'm so sorry," she said. Peter jumped off the couch and paced the room. He stopped and looked at a large picture frame on the mantle of the fireplace. It was a family photo of him and his parents. He picked it up and stared at the photo.

"You promised it'd all be fine. And now he's… where is he? I wanna see him!" He walked closer to her, with the picture frame in hand.

"The police have him."

"Police?! Where were they?"

"Peter…"

"Catch! It's Catch!" He threw the picture frame full force past Kayla and it shattered the window behind her. Kayla ducked as glass shards hit the cushions beside her. His eyes were wild, as he stormed out the back door.

"I'm so sorry," Kayla said. Peter's dad followed him, and his mom swept the floor.

"Please don't worry, Kayla. We'll get that. Just let us know if you need anything," she said.

A few days later, Josh performed the memorial service. Regina suggested having the service at a different location, but Kayla knew it had to be at Church on the Rock. All the children and their new families sat together on the front two rows. The history of this building had an impact on all of them. This place brought them all together again. Kayla's family sat to her right, but an empty seat remained on her left. Peter was also supposed to speak, but ran away from home the night before. She insisted his seat was held open for him. He was Will's brother, and she ached for him to be there. Rex gave kind words. There were many from the church in attendance. Several co-workers from The Denver Post brought flowers and sat together to support Kayla. Even in the context of such a dark past, this young man was given the highest regard of dignity. He was a hero to these children and these families. Many wept, especially the children. Kayla sat frozen, with her hands in her lap. She held tightly to the ultrasound picture, and rubbed it with her thumbs. Kayla couldn't look people directly in the eyes, and she spoke in a raspy whisper.

About a week after the tragedy, Pete Rivers came to the house. He expressed deep sorrow for the family's loss.

"The service was real nice, Kayla. And, of course, you can take off as much time as you need. Your job is here." She didn't look at her boss but gave a slight nod. He scratched the back of his head. "Kayla, this might not be a good time, but I just thought you should know. Well, remember a while back, I pressed you for the deadline on that trafficking article? Well, I did it because… well, I thought it was special. And I knew if it got in by New Year's then it would be eligible…" his voice dropped off. He could tell she wasn't really listening. She sat staring out the window. "Well, the West Coast Regionals, you know that award they give out every year. Lots of notoriety. Kayla, you won it." Her eyes looked toward his, but they were empty. Pete set down an invitation to the Annual West Coast Regionals luncheon on the coffee table in front of her. "I know this isn't a good time, but I just thought you should know."

May 1, 2010
SO WHAT !?! ??!??

Walking past Will's room was unbearable, and sometimes she found herself trapped in bed for fear of seeing his
empty room down the hallway. Other times she sat on his bed
and sobbed. One day Regina found Kayla fast asleep completely hidden in his covers. Kayla slept best when she could close
her eyes and pretend Will was by her side under the smell of
his sheets.

Dee Ann called Kayla every single day with encouraging words, scriptures, and prayers. Josh visited the house fre-
quently. He never brought Mattie. Kayla wasn't ready for Mattie
yet. Josh had a patient endurance that proved him faithful over
the recent months. Kayla bit her lip while she sat in the living
room with him.

"I killed him, Josh."

"What? Kayla, don't think that."

"I was so stupid. We should have just called the police.
Instead, I listened to Will; I did my own thing. Tried to be a
hero. Then that man saw my face, and Dad's. I am sure we were
on surveillance cameras at the hotel. A while back, Will told me
that I was in too deep. He pushed me away to protect me, and I
should be the one protecting him."

"You rescued those kids." Kayla's eyes burned and she

shook her head furiously.

"I let Will down. I couldn't help him," she said as her bottom lip quivered.

"Do you remember what he said to you the day he came home?" Kayla sat silently. "He said that he would rather have a mom, even if only for one day, than live the way he did before. You gave him the thing he had wanted his whole life. You gave him you. I watched Kayla. You have been transformed over the past year. You gave generously, and you didn't ask for anything back. You rearranged your whole life for him. Nobody else did that, but you did. You were a mom to him when nobody else would be. You didn't let him down. You picked him up."

Slow tears warmed her face. Josh was right, and after weeks of encouragement, she was actually starting to believe him, just a little. Later that night, Kayla sat on her bed, sorting through a pile of random papers that had been growing on the desk. Spread around her were receipts, junk mail, her picture with Will and the Christmas tree tied to her car, the awards luncheon invitation, and then her file from the clinic. She picked up the file and flipped through the pages. She focused on the handwritten receipt on the back of the last page. She remembered the night she found these cryptic notes, and her mind raced to the memories of the phone call with the DNA test results. *He's your son.* Then she remembered the metal cabinet in the church basement, and the hidden infant medical room. So many more files just like hers. So many more sons and daughters, who were stolen. So many children with no one to watch over them. These were the children of the city she had written about. These were children with no mother or father to stand up for them. And though her heart was still horribly broken, and she still missed her precious boy, something inside of her leapt. Someone had to care for these kids. And for the first time, she felt a gentle nudge from above saying: *You can do this. This is what I made you for. I made you to love them. I made you to love.*

"I'm in," Josh said. That morning Kayla had driven to the church to meet him. "All in. I told you I would be here, and I can feel it, Kayla. This is right." Kayla smiled softly. It had been weeks since she smiled.

"Will didn't want to leave any of those kids behind. He didn't want to let the silence enslave him anymore. And I think that if he was here to do it, he would." As Kayla opened a metal cabinet full of files, a sense of peace melted through all the tension that had gripped her body since Will died. She had carried most of the third-term procedure files from the basement out to her car. A remaining stash had been stored in Josh's office. There wasn't much time left to get prepared for her flight the next morning.

"I want you to come with me."

"Absolutely." Josh didn't hesitate. As Kayla packed files into a large suitcase, Josh made arrangements for Mattie and booked his airline ticket and hotel room. Despite the darkness that told her she was alone and would never be heard, she knew it was a lie.

With an armful of files, Kayla looked at Josh's office desk. A black wooden frame sat with a photo of Mattie's glowing face. Kayla smiled at the sparkling little eyes, but nearly lost her breath as Josh clumsily bumped into her with his hands full.

"Oh!" Kayla fumbled as she grabbed his desk to catch herself. A few files fell, which knocked over the picture frame.

"I'm so sorry," he apologized. She bent over, to grab the files, and then saw the frame on the floor. Mattie's picture had only been propped in front of the glass and had slipped out in the fall. Kayla gasped to see the original portrait displayed in the frame. A younger Josh with his arms around a pregnant woman smiled through the glass. She had wavy blonde curls, big blue eyes, and ivory skin with a few freckles. It was Carrie. Her long, lost friend from younger days.

"Carrie," she said, as though she meeting her friend with a warm embrace. She looked at Josh.

"My wife. And Mattie's mom," he said. "It was her idea to have this place be restored to a place of hope and faith. She died in childbirth with Mattie, and I knew that her dream for this place didn't die, too."

"But did you know...?"

"I have her file in my desk."

"She was my friend. She walked through all this with me." She looked at the picture of the young happy couple. "I have missed her."

"Me, too."

Kayla gave Josh some time to put his office back together and tend to a few phone calls in his office. Dee Ann walked Kayla to the car. Dee's arm wrapped around Kayla's shoulder. The sun was bright and a few humming birds buzzed by.

"He's a good man," Dee Ann said. This woman had grown as a source of comfort. Her wisdom was timely; her touch was soft and intuitive. Dee Ann wasn't quite old enough to be a mother to Kayla, and not young enough to be her sister either. In many ways, she was simply an angel who spoke life into the brokenness. Kayla nodded at Dee Ann's comment. "Sometimes I think I learn more about God, by what I see in that man's conviction. God has built in him a pure heart, a gentle heart. He's faithful." Kayla nodded again. "Most people can't see it, but I know that Josh still has a ring on his finger. At least in his heart."

"He is a great friend. I've learned a lot from him," Kayla said. Dee Ann nodded back. It took a few more hugs before Kayla drove off.

That was the first night Kayla didn't cry. Her son had helped her see something new. Kayla Barrington had always believed in destiny, but never believed she could be part of something bigger than herself. Until today. Josh and Kayla arrived at the University of Southern California with a heavy rolling suitcase behind them. Flowers were in bloom, and fountains splashed in the reflection ponds all around campus. Josh took a picture of Kayla next to the Trojan mascot statue. A bright blue sky met the HOLLYWOOD sign and mountainous horizon. They were not distracted by the luxury of Los Angeles. Everyone in the room noticed their inner strength. Government officials, community dignitaries, and the press gathered in the ballroom. They sat at round tables covered in white linens and silver-plated finery. Bundles of pink roses were arranged at the center of each table.

It was a pinnacle moment for Kayla, but not because of a medal, or prize money, or the honor achieved. For so long, a fog of self-ambition had blinded her sights. Now, all was clear, and she was ready to embrace a new life of purpose. Stepping up to the microphone, she graciously received her award and silently gave a thankful prayer as she looked out to the audience. Nodding at Josh, he walked toward the stage pulling a suitcase behind him.

"In the mid eighteen hundreds, our nation was at odds. Less than one hundred years before, the United States of America was established by people who believed in the power of freedom. Our founding fathers had a vision that this country would be like no other. They dreamed that we would be a body of people, not united by the boundaries of our land, but united by the convictions in our hearts. They believed that we would shine brightly to the rest of the world because, as a nation, we would value humanity. We would treasure people, whether rich or poor, strong or weak, man or woman, or any race. We esteem them all to be one of us. Yet, in the mid eighteen hundreds, our country was being torn apart, and finally at war over this fact. Are we willing to care about people? Are we willing to love them, and defend the innocent? Will our country be a safe place for all who call this land their home? I am thankful for people like Harriet Tubman, James Fairfield, Thomas Garrett, and Frederick Douglass who pioneered the Underground Railroad. I am thankful for leaders like Abraham Lincoln, Ulysses S. Grant, and the many others who fought for the union of our country. They, and many others, believed that freedom was worth fighting for.

"Today, America is not at odds. We are asleep. Time has passed, and darkness has crept in under our noses without hardly a notice. Slavery has returned to our land, but now the slaves are the ones trapped underground. Human trafficking generates $32 billion annually[3], and enslaves 30 million people around the globe,[4] half of them are children under the age of eighteen.[5] Modern day slavery is the second largest criminal industry in the world.[6] The industry profits rank second to the illegal drug trade and is expected to soon surpass it. Basically,

---

3    International Labor Office, A Global Alliance Against Forced Labor, Global Report Under the Follow-up to the ILO Declaration on Fundamental Principles and Rights at Work, Geneva: 2005), 55, http://www.ilo.org/global/publications/ilo-bookstore/order-online/books/WCMS_081882/lang--en/index.htm (accessed December 9, 2010).
4    http://www.globalslaveryindex.org
5    U.S. Department of State, Trafficking in Persons Report, 7th ed. (Washington, DC: U.S. Department of State, 2007), 8.
6    http://www.notforsalecampaign.org/about/slavery/

people are realizing that you can only sell crack cocaine once and it is gone, but you can exploit a child over and over and over. It is a much more lucrative business. Human trafficking occurs whenever a person is forced into labor, services, or sexual exploitation for the profit of the traffickers."

Josh began stacking the medical files on a table next to Kayla's podium. The pile grew, and the audience was captivated by the fateful sound of the heavy papers. Kayla picked up a few of the files in her hand.

"These are some of the children in Denver, Colorado, who have been trafficked, abused, raped, and pillaged for someone's evil gain." She put the files back down. "Denver. Did you catch that? We're not talking about some impoverished country. Without question, the depravity in other countries is great. The need for rescue is real. But the darkness has come to our land. It is estimated that 300,000 prostituted children are living on the streets in the United States ever year.[7] And there's almost no way of knowing how many adults within our borders are enslaved today. There are those trafficked in across borders, those taken out, and those in our very midst." Kayla paused. Her throat grew tight. She swallowed deeply and stood tall. A slide show of pictures began to play on the large screen behind her. First were investigation photos of the Green House and the filthy rooms, sex toys, and stained blood on the carpets.

"It is a scary life for a person enslaved. For them, the world is dark. For them, there is no hope. No one hears their cries. Their spirits have been crushed. Their bodies have been invaded and torn to pieces. They have been manipulated, threatened, beaten, tortured, and terrified. They have been

---

7    ECPAT International, "Europe and North America Regional Profile," End Child Prostitution, Child Pornography, and the Trafficking of Children for Sex, (Stockholm: World Congress Against the Commercial Sexual Exploitation against Children, 1996), 70, http://www.csecworldcongress.org/en/stockholm/Reports/Regional_Workshops.htm (accessed December 9, 2010).

brainwashed into believing that no one cares and that they are utterly worthless." Photos of the different children from the Green House slowly appeared on the screen.

"And these are not just numbers. These are not just faceless statistics we can ignore. These are precious babies, children, teenagers, and adults. They have no one to call their father or mother. These children belong to no one, but the city." The last picture remained on the screen. It was of Will and Kayla standing next to their Christmas tree in the grocery store parking lot. "I have to be honest, I have spent most of my life worrying about me. My life, my success, my fun. And it wasn't until I had to look one of these boys in the eyes, and realize…" her eyes watered, and her voice cracked. "He is mine." Her lip quivered as she looked down at the podium. "He was mine. But there are so many others out there. Many who need you, who need me. They need *us*… to care. This is not the time to sleep. This is not the time to roll over with a jaded attitude toward justice. It is time to act." She looked at Josh standing on the side of the stage. "Silence will not win. We are ready. I am ready to step up and make this country what it was designed to be. A people who believe in, die for, and fight for… freedom. I am ready."

# APPENDIX: RISING UP TODAY

*How can you help stop human trafficking?*

## AWARENESS:

Above all, people must know. This novel has been written to aide you with a tool to share with others. You can host a book club, or prompt others in the community to promote awareness. Use your own creative efforts to shed light on this darkness. People cannot help if they do not know.

## JOIN OR HOST A BOOK CLUB:

This may be one of the easiest ways you can tell others about human trafficking. This book introduces the topics and research, and a book club opens the door for discussion igniting passion and action. Check out ChildrenOfTheCityBook.com to learn more about how to join or host your own book club.

## BE WATCHFUL:

Keep your mind alert to situations around you. If you see adults or children that look suspicious or susceptible, take note of surrounding details and call the hotline immediately. Take pictures with your phone to help you remember details or submit to law enforcement. View the list of "Signs of Human Trafficking" on pages 226-227.

## HUMAN TRAFFICKING HELP-LINE:

Save this phone number, and call or text to report any suspicious activity. Available 24/7: National Human Trafficking Resource Center: 888-373-7888, or Text HELP or INFO to BE FREE (233733)

## START A LOCAL TASK FORCE:

Meet on a monthly basis and build unity in the marketplace, educational system, local church, and law enforcement. Work together to bring awareness and educational opportunities to your city.

## AMAZON'S SMILE PROGRAM:

When you sign in through Smile.Amazon.com, you can designate an organization to receive a percentage of Amazon's profits from every purchase you make! It's such an easy way to contribute, and many of the organizations listed below can receive these benefits.

## CONNECT:

There are many great non-profit organizations that strive to end human slavery. Each one utilizes different avenues and strategies to make an impact. You can give financially, volunteer, join an internship, or contact the organization personally for ideas on how to help accomplish their goals. Below is a list of trusted organizations that work in different ways to stop human slavery.

### THE A-21 CAMPAIGN

thea21campaign.org    Twitter: @TheA21Campaign

The A-21 Campaign is an international anti-human trafficking organization with the goal of abolishing slavery in the 21st century. A-21 aims for prevention, protection, prosecution, and partnerships. They have admin offices, field offices and restoration locations in Australia, Europe, Africa, and the United States.

### HAND OF HOPE

joycemeyer.org/handofhope

Hand of Hope supports children' homes, feeding programs, medical aide, and inner city work. They also rescue trafficked women and children in the United States, India, Ethiopia, Cambodia, Thailand, Bulgaria, Ukraine, Greece, and Lesotho. For survivors, Hand of Hope offers love, housing, schooling, job skill training, and counseling to rebuild and restore lives.

## END IT MOVEMENT

enditmovement.com    Twitter: @EnditMovement
Awareness and action are the primary goals while connecting people with organizations. End It Movement calls everyone to raise their voice; they often provide mass awareness opportunities to join involving social media and video.

## RESTORE ONE

restoreonelife.org    Twitter: @RestoreOne
Restore One seeks to open shelters offering faith-based and proven clinical methods for restoration to American boys. They are currently the only shelter in the U.S.A. offering aide to trafficked boys specifically.

## IEMPATHIZE

iempathize.org    Twitter: @iEmpathize
iEmpathize works to eradicate child exploitation on a global level and engage culture in creative solutions. They empower the kids, sectors, and regions most effected by the issue. They constantly host awareness events filled with creative imagery and sensory designed to evoke empathy and compassion.

## THE POLARIS PROJECT

polarisproject.org    Twitter: @Polaris_Project
Based in the U.S. and Japan, Polaris Project works to advance state and federal policy related to the crime of human trafficking. Passing strong legislation creates protection for victims and accountability for traffickers and others contributing to human trafficking.

## SAK SAUM

saksaum.com

Located in Cambodia, Sak Saum rescues and restores exploited women and men. They facilitate vocational training empowering victims to completely step away from their dark past. Sak Saum offers an online store featuring trendy accessories produced by survivors which provide sustainable income for a life of freedom. You can donate, purchase, or share on Pinterest.

## ABOLITION INTERNATIONAL

abolitioninternational.org     Twitter: @AbolitionIntl

Founded by singer/songwriter, Natalie Grant, Abolition International works to end sexual slavery through quality aftercare, accreditation, advocacy, and awareness.

## RESTORE INNOCENCE

restoreinnocence.org     Twitter: @restoreblackbow

Restore Innocence works with women rescued out of exploitation in America. They host "Cinderella's House" as a safe home for recovery, provide mentoring programs, and fill "Restore Bags" for children pulled off the streets. When a victim is rescued in a sting operation, everything on their body is considered "evidence." Restore Bags contain brand-new items such as clothing, products for personal hygiene, and snacks. These are given directly to police to administer and help create a relationship of trust between the victims and law enforcement officials.

You can serve and bring Restore Bags to your state, too!

## PEARL ALLIANCE

messengerinternational.org     Twitter: @PearlAlliance

Messenger International has a raid and rescue outreach called Pearl Alliance targeting brothels, pedophile homes, arrest for child pornography, and other advances against human trafficking in South East Asia.

# THE EXODUS ROAD

theexodusroad.com     Twitter: @TheExodusRoad

The Exodus Road coalition empowers rescue by advocating in the field of counter-trafficking with three characteristics: Operating in SouthEast Asia, Targeted Interventions (Investigations, Raids, Prosecutions) and After-Care.

# INTERNATIONAL JUSTICE MISSION

ijm.org     Twitter: @IJM

IJM has a mission to rescue thousands, protect millions, and prove that justice for the poor is possible. With 16 field offices around the world, more than 500 lawyers, investigators, social workers and staff work to secure tangible and sustainable protection of national laws through local court systems. IJM was highlighted by U.S. News and World Report as one of the top 10 nonprofits "making a difference."

# GIRLS AGAINST PORN AND HUMAN TRAFFICKING

http://girlsagainstporn.com     Twitter: @GAPGal1

This activist group educates on obscenity laws. There are many laws prohibiting the distribution of pornography and GAP&HT advocates on behalf of citizens to ensure that current laws in place are enforced. There are incredible ways to get involved with GAP&HT locally in your community.

# BEAUTIFUL AND BELOVED

beautifulandbeloved.com     Twitter: @BeautifulBelovd

The store endeavors to drive global job creation in the fair trade industry through the sale of items created by newly empowered survivors of slavery and people previously marginalized. Through your purchase, you can support the mission of other nonprofits around the world that are making a difference.

## SIGNS OF HUMAN TRAFFICKING

Awareness is not just for a rally or event, it is intended to open our eyes so that we can see things happening in our own cities. Take note of the following signs, and you might have the opportunity to make a difference in someone's life.

*Do you encounter a person with any of these traits?*

## INFORMATION FROM SHARED HOPE:

- Significantly older boyfriend
- Signs of Trauma (physical or other)
- Traveling with an older male (not guardian)
- Chronic runaway
- Multiple Delinquent charges
- Homelessness
- Special Marked tattoos

## ADDITIONAL INFORMATION FROM THE POLARIS PROJECT:

*Common Work and Living Conditions:*
- Is not free to leave or come and go as he/she wishes
- Is under 18 and is providing commercial sex acts
- Is in the commercial sex industry under a pimp/manager
- Is unpaid, paid very little, or paid only through tips
- Works excessively long and/or unusual hours
- Is not allowed breaks, suffers unusual restrictions at work
- Owes a large debt and is unable to pay it off
- Was recruited through false promises concerning the nature and conditions of his/her work
- High security measures exist in the work and/or living locations (e.g. opaque windows, boarded up windows, bars on windows, barbed wire, security cameras, etc.)
- Poor Mental Health or Abnormal Behavior

- Is fearful, anxious, depressed, overly submissive, tense, or nervous/paranoid
- Exhibits unusually fearful or anxious behavior after bringing up law enforcement
- Avoids eye contact

## *Poor Physical Health*
- Lacks health care
- Appears malnourished
- Shows signs of physical and/or sexual abuse, physical restraint, confinement, or torture
- Lack of Control
- Has few or no personal possessions
- Is not in control of his/her own money, no financial records, or bank account
- Is not in control of his/her own identification documents (ID or passport)
- Is not allowed or able to speak for themselves (a third party may insist on being present and/or translating)

## *Other*
- Claims of just visiting and inability to clarify where he/she is staying/address
- Lack of knowledge of whereabouts and/or do not know what city he/she is in
- Loss of sense of time
- Has numerous inconsistencies in his/her story

*To learn more, visit: sharedhope.org or polarisproject.org.*

# A QUICK LOOK AT THE STATISTICS:

*What is human trafficking?*
Human Trafficking is the recruitment, smuggling, transporting, harboring, buying or selling of a person through force, threats, fraud, deception, or coercion for the purposes of exploitation, prostitution, pornography, migrant work, sweat shops, domestic servitude, forced labor, bondage, peonage or involuntary servitude.

- 29.8 million people are held in slavery world wide.[8]
- Human Trafficking generates a $32 billion dollar criminal industry. [9]
- 80% of the victims are women, and HALF are children under the age of 18.[10]
- 800,000-900,000 people are trafficked across international borders each year.[11]

## IN AMERICA:

- It is estimated that 300,000 prostituted children are living on the streets in America.[12]
- 50,000 people are trafficked into the U.S.A. each year.[13]
- 2,300 children go missing each day. 50% are expected to end up sexual exploitation.[14]

---

8    http://www.globalslaveryindex.org
9    International Labor Office, A Global Alliance Against Forced Labor, Global Report Under the Follow-up to the ILO Declaration on Fundamental Principles and Rights at Work, (Geneva: 2005), 55, http://www.ilo.org/global/publications/ilo-bookstore/order-online/books/WCMS_081882/lang--en/index.htm (accessed December 9, 2010).
10    U.S. Department of State, Trafficking in Persons Report, 7th ed. (Washington, DC: U.S. Department of State, 2007), 8.
11    U.S. Department of State, Trafficking in Persons Report, 8th ed. (Washington, DC: U.S. Department of State, 2008), 7.
12    ECPAT International, "Europe and North America Regional Profile," End Child Prostitution, Child Pornography, and the Trafficking of Children for Sex, (Stockholm: World Congress Against the Commercial Sexual Exploitation against Children, 1996), 70, http://www.csecworldcongress.org/en/stockholm/Reports/Regional_Workshops.htm (accessed December 9, 2010).
13    Amy O'Neill Richard, International Trafficking in Women to the United States: A Contemporary Manifestation of Slavery and Organized Crime, Center for the Study of Intelligence, November 1999, p. iii.
14    http://www.crimelibrary.com/criminal_mind/forensics/americas_missing/2.html
        http://www.childfindofamerica.org/information.htm

- 70% of reported underage victims were in the foster system.[15]
- 1.68 million children run away from home each year.[16]
- In one Chicago based study, traffickers sold anywhere from 20-800 individual women in their lifetime.[17]
- 95% of all commercial sex engaged in by boys is provided to adult males.[18]
- Buyers reported that they were an average of 21 years of age when they first bought sex.[19]
- 48% of men view pornography once a week or more often.[20]

## BOOKS TO READ:

Not For Sale // By David Batstone
Good News About Injustice // By Gary A. Haugan
Priceless: A Novel on the Edge of the World // By Tom Davis

## MOVIES AND MEDIA:

Nefarious: Merchant of Souls // nefariousdocumentary.com
CHOSEN // By Shared Hope // sharedhope.org

## ADDITIONAL REPORTS:

**Congressional Research Service**
www.fas.org/sgp/crs/row/RL34317.pdf

**Polaris Project Human Trafficking Statistics**
www.handsacrosstheworldmn.org/resources/Human+Trafficking+Statistics.pdf

**Shared Hope**
http://sharedhope.org/wp-content/uploads/2013/11/DMSTinfographic.pdf

**Federal Bureau of Investigation**
http://www.fbi.gov/about-us/investigate/civilrights/human_trafficking

15   http://www.wyden.senate.gov/download/?id=e495e784-6ebc-426c-b88d-205f0e498ec9&download=1
16   http://www.missingkids.com/en_US/documents/nismart2_overview.pdf
17   http://newsroom.depaul.edu/PDF/FAMILY_LAW_CENTER_REPORT-final.pdf
18   Richard J. Estes and Neil A. Weiner. The Commercial Sexual Exploitation of Children in the U.S., Canada, and Mexico, (The University of Pennsylvania School of Social Work: 2001), 128.
19   http://sharedhope.org/wp-content/uploads/2013/11/DMSTinfographic.pdf
20   http://www.prostitutionresearch.com/pdfs/Farleyetal2011ComparingSexBuyers.pdf

## IN-PERSON IMPACT:

In January 2014, hundreds of people came together and supported *CHILDREN of the CITY*. It was a book they had never read, written by a girl who had never published. They saw the vision, cared for the cause, and united as a people. We extend humble gratitude to all who gave and special recognition to the sacrificial investment of those listed below.

## FREEDOM FIGHTER:

Milton and Donna Sue Armstrong
Dan and Laura Barnett
Bill and Connie Bookwalter
Jeff and Janice Clift
Steve and Thea Corder
James and Jane Eggstaff
Marc and Debbie Forcier
Dr. Scott and Sally Fairchild
Thaddeus and Kari House
Dr. Dean and Mary Lohse
Alyse Jacobsen & Brett Heinz
Emmett and Tasha Mitchell
Planet Smoothie, The Avenue Viera
Planet Smoothie/Tasti D Lite
Rick and Jeanette Roach
George and Linda Richardson
Michael and Susan Stephens
Justin and Meagan Sternberg
Michael and Jennifer Stevens
Michael and Brittany Woodside
Faith Fellowship Church Youth Ministry
Dan and Charity Schaefer // TCB-Elite Limited

Joe and Laura Arant
Chris and Jenna Carberg
Jim and Judy Coleman
Ryan Collipi
Joe and Desire Cruz
Mary Anne Fisher
Dan Gore
Andrew and Brenna Hoy
Jeffrey and Jessie Hoy
In Memory of Dean Kuna
Melissa Paddock
Hank and Susan Manalli
Ralph and Clarola Reeves
Bernard and Julie Salcedo
Mike and Denise Rice
Pete and Cathy Sterling
Luke and Cheri Thomas
Whitney Ward
Mickey and Brenda Weed
Zach Yocum

## ABOLITIONIST:

Baby Hope
Holly Gardner
Josh and Kendyl Haagan
Brian and Anastacia Hawkins-Smith
Autumn Lawler
Dr. Ruben and Rita Moreno
Jesse and Kristin Wallace
Dr. David and Ginny Whitley

## RESCUE SQUAD:

Faith Fellowship Academy

Dr. Jeffrey and Ann Hoy

Bob and Janet Whitmire

Mary Kay Unit #145
marykay.com/angelawhite
*"Blessed is she who believed in the fulfillment of what had
been spoken to her by the Lord."* –Luke 1:45

Love Ablaze
loveablaze.com

## REVOLUTIONARY:

Cruise and Crop Cruises
www.cruiseandcrop.com

*Special Thanks to: Rhetorik, Dan Gore, and Rob Burrell for your
amazing creative work on the book trailer!*

## ABOUT THE AUTHOR:

TIFFANY PASTOR is a dreamer with a relentless passion for helping people. She is a polished public speaker who encourages and casts vision with boldness. As a Theatre major and alumni of the University of Central Florida, Tiffany utilizes the art of storytelling and dramatic dynamics to captivate her audience. After years of writing, speaking, leadership development, and graphic design, Tiffany is thrilled to bring it all together and share her first published novel, as a powerful awareness tool. She is honored to serve as a Next Generation Pastor with her husband, while investing in stronger families, children, youth, and 20somethings at their local church.

## BEHIND THE STORY:

Would you like to know more about the research behind this story? Visit childrenofthecitybook.com/behind-the-story to learn more.

## THE GOALS OF CHILDREN OF THE CITY

> To be an AWARENESS TOOL for people to share.
> To INCITE ACTION and connect readers to non-profits.
> DONATE 40% of all author royalties to anti-slavery organizations.

## CHILDRENOFTHECITYBOOK.COM

# FREEDOM FIGHTER GUIDE
### ⟩⟩⟩ TAKE A DEEPER LOOK AT CHILDREN OF THE CITY

This interactive resource is full of survivor stories, statistics, and teaching that inspires practical application in the fight to end slavery at the local and global level. Get your copy of the Freedom Fighter Guide to build rich small group discussion, or simply read on your own.

**AVAILABLE AT AMAZON.COM**

# HOW WILL YOU SHARE THE STORY?

**BOOK CLUBS**

**A GIFT TO OTHERS**

**EVENTS**

**FREEDOM FIGHTER GUIDE**

**SOCIAL MEDIA**

TEENAGERS ARE THE PRIME TARGET.

PREVENT AND PROTECT AS YOU SHARE THE STORY!

*HAVE*
# TIFFANY PASTOR
>>> *SPEAK AT YOUR EVENT.*

Tiffany is dedicated to speaking life into the lives of young people, women, and multi-generational groups. Visit the website below to have her join your event, retreat, or ministry.

**CHILDRENOFTHECITYBOOK.COM**